The Ultimate Holiday

Andrew Kraft

This is a work of fiction. Names, characters, places, and incidents either are the product of the author's imagination or are used fictitiously. Any resemblance to actual persons, living or dead, events, or locales is entirely coincidental.

Copyright © 2023 by Andrew Kraft

All rights reserved. No part of this book may be reproduced in any form on by an electronic or mechanical means, including information storage and retrieval systems, without permission in writing from the publisher, except by a reviewer who may quote brief passages in a review.

First Edition: March 2023

ISBN 979-8-3784-7643-5

CONTENTS

Preface	Preface	Pg #1
Chapter 1	Iceland	Pg #5
Chapter 2	Mexico	Pg #31
Chapter 3	Cuba	Pg #43
Chapter 4	Romania	Pg #51
Chapter 5	Switzerland	Pg #57
Chapter 6	Colombia	Pg #69
Chapter 7	Sweden	Pg #79
Chapter 8	Canada	Pg #87
Chapter 9	Dominican Republic	Pg #99
Chapter 10	Spain	Pg #111
Chapter 11	Australia	Pg #119
Chapter 12	New Zealand	Pg #133
Chapter 13	England	Pg #145
Chapter 14	Germany	Pg #153
Chapter 15	Netherlands	Pg #163
Chapter 16	Hungary	Pg #175
Extras	Author's Note	Pg #189

Preface

Before you read this book, I would like you to know I have been to each of these beautiful countries and loved my experience in every one of them. I visited these places around the time listed in the book and wondered, what could go terribly wrong in each of these locations? Some of these stories are things I've seen or experienced and thought about where it could lead if taken to the extreme. Many of the conversations are ones I was a part of, and I want to share my weird sense of humor and odd things I've learned about other cultures around the world.

Traveling has given me an incredible world view and grasp on different perspectives, and I encourage everyone to do the same. I have spent most of my life valuing experiences over personal possessions, and I don't regret living that way. One thought that has always haunted me is lying on my deathbed and realizing I spent all my time working to afford physical things and not experiencing everything this amazing world has to offer.

I hope this book does alright, so I can continue to have experiences like the ones I had on my quest to visit thirty countries before I turned thirty. I have either been to or have plans to visit six of the seven continents while writing this book, and I hope to earn the money to afford the super expensive Antarctica experience one day. I've always dreamed about traveling on one of these thirteen-hour flights in first class, so maybe I can finally make that dream a reality with book sales. It's too late to fund first class for my next fourteen-hour flight to South Africa and for an even longer journey over to South Korea and Japan, but maybe the next one after those.

I intertwined some of the stories in this collection and there is a rollercoaster of emotions and experiences that I think flow well, so I would recommend reading them in order. However, the stories can be read in any order, and you can jump around to places you have been to or might currently live in to get a glimpse of what I learned while I was there. These stories either have some lessons or are simply a fun way to exaggerate the cultures I have experienced over my years of traveling. These experiences have given me a wealth I could have never imagined. I'm hoping one day, I'll look back on life and say that I didn't waste my time here on this small blue orb floating through the great vastness of our universe.

I hope the reader has fun experiencing the world through my partial experiences here and isn't discouraged from exploring any of these wonderful countries for themselves. Me writing this is proof that I made it back safely from each country, and I would go back to any of them if given the chance. Many folks in the United States only hear the bad stories from other countries, however, I have felt safer in most of these places than in my hometown of

THE ULTIMATE HOLIDAY

Baltimore, Maryland. If you're reading this b(
way to one of these amazing countries, you mig
avoid that chapter until you're back home safely.

Iceland

(September 2015)

'Twas the night before Jeff departed for Iceland and, per usual, he packed his bags that evening. Although he had taken some domestic flights from his home in Fredericksburg, Virginia, he was still new to traveling and wanted to start the second-quarter century of his life with a trip to a foreign land. Jeff had been on a cruise the year before and got a crisp new passport since he planned to leave the country by plane, eventually.

His friend, Randy, had posted a tweet asking anyone if they wanted to travel to Iceland with him and his father, Jim. Jeff decided to go for it. He hung out with Randy a handful of times through mutual friends but had never met his father. It would probably surprise most of their mutual friends that they were all traveling together internationally. This was worrisome for Jeff, but he wasn't getting any younger and none of his close friends were providing the opportunity of a lifetime like this. Although a domestic trip would have been preferred for their first traveling experience together, he threw caution to the wind and trusted Randy abroad.

Packing before a vacation was always a daunting task for Jeff. He thought about the travel checklists he read about online as he stared at his luggage. The first thing on each checklist was to place your passport somewhere safe and secure so it would make it to the airport with you.

Jeff went directly to where he had stored his passport after returning from his cruise. He opened his bedroom closet and unlatched his document box that held his most secure belongings. His heart sank. It wasn't where it was supposed to be, in the front next to his checkbook. A knot formed in the pit of his stomach.

Jeff pulled out all the documents, making sure it hadn't slipped among his other folders inside. His passport was not there. He checked the other important documents like his social security card next to his pants in the dresser drawer, second from the top. Not there either. He ripped clothes out of every drawer and tore apart his entire bedroom, looking for his passport. To no avail.

After his room looked like the aftermath of a violent tornado had ripped through it, the thought dawned on him. Instead of placing his passport where he always kept it, Jeff had left it in his backpack after the cruise ship vacation, the only time he had been outside of the country and needed his passport. The same backpack stolen from his car's passenger side after he parked near Fells Point in Baltimore City when he traveled there for work the previous month.

The pendulum had swung completely in the other direction. Jeff had been researching Iceland for months, only to have his hopes and dreams ripped away from him in an instant. He could have avoided it if he had put his passport away after he got back from the cruise terminal, like his father had told him. Jeff felt like he was in college all over again having his professor scold him for waiting until the last night to start on a project and submit it past the deadline. Only this time, it would result in missing the vacation of a lifetime instead of the C+ in differential equations when he could have gotten a B-.

While mourning the death of his vacation, Jeff did what he always did when he had no clue what to do next. He called his mother.

"Mom, there isn't anything I can do. My flight is tomorrow night, and I don't have a passport. I should have listened to dad after the cruise. He's always right with these kinds of things."

"I know how much you wanted to go on this vacation so you can't give up." His mother replied in a tone only a caring mother could use. "You're a problem solver, think about what you can control in this situation."

"Everything in this situation is completely out of my control."

"What time does the passport office close? How about you call the passport office and see if there is any way that they can help you? It doesn't hurt to ask."

"No one has ever gotten a passport within this amount of time before leaving the country. They would probably think I'm some sort of international criminal."

"You don't know until you try. They're probably closing soon. I'm going to hang up now, and you're going to start problem solving."

"Can you call them for me like when you called the dentist and set up my appointments for me?"

"*I'm* going to hang up now. *You're* going to start problem solving."

Tears welled up in Jeff's eyes. "You're the best mom I've ever had."

There was an extended silence and Jeff looked down at his phone to see if she had already hung up.

"I'm the *only* mom you've ever had, which also means I'm the worst. I love you. Bye."

Jeff's mom hung up before he could reply. He looked up the phone number and hours of operation for the passport office. Fifteen minutes left before they closed. It was a miracle. He frantically dialed the number and waited for someone to pick up after clicking on all the prompts that felt like they were going to take him past their closing time.

"Hello, this is Trina. How may I assist you today?"

"Hi, my name is Jeff. I'm really down on my luck right now. I'm hoping you can help me out."

"We'll certainly try. What's going on, Jeff?"

"I am leaving for Iceland tomorrow night, and I just remembered someone recently stole my backpack that had my passport in it. What are my options here?"

"That's some bad luck there. You know what they say, it's better to have bad luck than no luck at all."

"Who's they? That doesn't make me feel much better."

"Let me see what we can do for you. Please hold on."

Jeff paced back and forth in his bedroom, waiting for what he knew he would certainly hear. He wasn't boarding the flight to Iceland. Jeff had spent at least a thousand dollars at this point and countless hours planning this trip, all for nothing. He had already taken off from work the following week and had spent the whole previous week bragging about the trip to make his coworkers jealous. Jeff was *not* going to spend precious vacation days sitting at home. Now he was going to have to walk into work each day next week with his tail between his legs, hoping they wouldn't make fun of him too much.

The hold tone ceased, and Trina came back on the line.

"Someone upstairs must be looking out for you because I've never seen this happen before."

"I like the sound of that!" Hope burst through Jeff. There was a brief pause as Trina pecked away at her keyboard. "Tell me more, Trina. The suspense is killing me."

"We have an appointment for tomorrow morning at nine a.m. available."

"So, you're saying I'm going to make it to Iceland?"

"It's only an appointment. You still have to make your way to D.C. tomorrow morning and convince an agent that you need this passport the same day."

"This is incredible!"

"Bring your documentation and proof of your booked flight with you tomorrow."

"Thank you so much for your help."

Jeff gave Trina his information and hung up the phone. He felt like the luckiest boy in the entire world. He had gotten all the way to the edge of the cliff of defeat, and was talked off the ledge by his mother and managed to get a fighting chance. He packed the rest of his bags with the clothes he had tossed all over the floor and figured out his schedule for the following day. He needed to get a passport photo and stop by his work office to print his flight information, since he didn't have a printer at home. Then he had to convince one of Trina's coworkers to let him get a same-day passport. Piece of cake.

Jeff woke up at four a.m. after getting only an hour of sleep. He stayed up stressing most of the night about the day ahead of him. Numerous pieces had to come together. Jeff was sanguine, hoping everything would work out and he would be in Iceland tomorrow morning.

The roads were clear at that hour, and Jeff drove as if no cops were on duty either. His car had been in hundreds of pieces countless times the previous summer as he modified it to go faster than it should. Jeff was testing out those modifications this morning. He almost struck a person who was running by the parking lot entrance to the drugstore as he pulled in. Who even runs that early anyway? Absolute psychopaths, that's who.

He ran into the store like he was trying to purchase lottery tickets with his lucky numbers right before the big drawing. Jeff looked around and didn't see anyone behind the counter. He patiently waited for a couple minutes assuming someone would notice him on the security cameras or that he tripped a sensor or something. Nothing. He walked aisle to aisle, hoping to find someone stocking shelves with their headphones on not paying attention. No one around, he could steal anything he wanted. There was only one thing he needed right now though. Jeff heard a door creaking near the front of the store.

"Hey man, can I help you with something?" the store employee said.

"There you are. Where have you been?" Jeff asked as if he was interrogating him for a heinous crime.

"Night shift is tough. I fall asleep in the back sometimes."

"I could have robbed everything in this place before you came out."

"Thanks for not doing that. Do you need something?"

"A passport photo, please."

Jeff hastily left the drugstore and didn't bother holding the door for the same lady he almost struck in his car earlier. What was she doing? Running laps around the place waiting for him? The store did have cold beverages and a bathroom; it was probably a solid running pitstop. He drove off for his work office, with much more traffic on the road. Jeff weaved in and out of cars and kept his little racecar speedometer in the double digits this time.

It was still early and he hoped to avoid talking to any of his coworkers. The only person there was Rick, his boss. Jeff crept through the office, ducking his head below the cubicle walls. He logged in and typed as quietly as he could and clicked print. The printer, which was outside of his boss's office, howled like it was a dial-up internet connection from the early 2000s. Rick walked out of his office and picked up Jeff's flight confirmation when a voice from far away interrupted him.

"Rick!"

"Steve! Who let you in here?" Rick asked.

Rick put Jeff's flight confirmation papers on top of the printer and walked over to go meet his old buddy. Jeff slipped by where they were standing in the aisle and grabbed his paperwork like an assassin who had been training all his life for this one job. He hopped in his car and sped off without any delays. This day was going too perfectly.

Traffic had picked up, and Jeff wished he would have been on his motorcycle so he could split lanes in between cars. Jeff would take his motorcycle, weather permitting, whenever he was running behind schedule to shave time off his commute. His luggage definitely would not have fit on his bike though. Jeff was going to be devastated if he didn't leave early enough and traffic was the reason for not making his nine a.m. appointment. A few hours remained, but every second he sat in traffic was absolute torture.

Jeff had every parking garage mapped out in the area to ensure his success and had finally pulled into his first choice, with plenty of time to spare. He had never been in a parking garage like this that didn't have directions on where to go. His car crawled through until a man jogging alongside him knocked on his window.

"Where are you going? Put your car in park and we'll take it from there," the employee said.

"Do you park my car for me? Can you drive a stick?"

"Yes, and yes. Have you ever left your house before? Don't you know what a valet is?"

"Alright. Take care of my car, her name is Maggie. I know exactly how many miles she has on her."

Jeff reluctantly gave his key to the employee after taking it off the key ring. He was always nervous about letting anyone take his car since it was fast and there was always the chance it would come back with extra miles on it. Jeff didn't have time to contemplate the situation.

With his passport picture in hand, Jeff stormed into the passport office with the confidence of a used car sales associate heading onto the lot to make his sales quota for the month.

"Your flight is tonight out of Dulles? I think we can get you on the plane."

"If you weren't on the other side of this plexiglass, I would kiss you on the mouth, my good sir," Jeff said.

"That's certainly not going to help you get on the flight."

"Or maybe just a firm handshake."

"Nope. Not that either. Come back after four p.m. and your passport should be ready. You will have plenty of time before your overnight flight."

"Perfect! Thank you so much!"

Jeff spent the day seeing the tourist attractions that he hadn't seen since the school field trip he took in the fifth grade. The Lincoln Memorial, the Washington Monument, the Vietnam Veterans Memorial, and he even had time to grab some food at the oldest restaurant in the city. Everything about this day was going perfectly. Jeff made his way back to the passport office after frolicking around town. He received his brand-new passport with the photo of him which looked like he had stayed up all night worrying about not getting his passport in time. It was the most successful day.

Jeff drove to meet his buddy Randy and his father Jim before they headed over to IAD. Jim had a house in Arlington where they would meet to call their taxi to get to the airport. Jeff got there before Randy, which was awkward, but it wasn't long before Randy arrived. They were standing in Jim's driveway waiting for the airport taxi, with luggage scattered all over the driveway.

"I'm so excited to use the luggage my parents bought me for this trip." Jeff was overtalking as he always did whenever he was excited and nervous. "It's the first time I've used them. My parents were embarrassed to be around me on our cruise with my old ratty bookbag and duffel bag. They bought me green luggage because they know green is my favorite color. They told me it would be easy to pick it out on the luggage carousel once we arrive."

Jim and Randy turned and looked at each other quizzically.

"You know your luggage is brown, right?" Randy asked.

"Now is probably a good time to let you know I'm partially red-green colorblind."

"Green is your favorite color, and you can't even see it?" Jim asked.

"I'm partially colorblind. I can see green. It's probably duller than what you see."

Jeff had been a Baltimore Ravens fan for most of his

life and was never able to truly appreciate their team color, purple. He lived closer to the Washington football team stadium but could never root for that terrible organization.

"Now we know that," Randy replied. "We also know your parents hate you and lied to you."

"Well, they didn't tell me it was green. I guess I assumed, and I thought they were green."

"Brown is slightly easier to tell apart from the sea of black luggage, I suppose." Jim added to make Jeff feel better about his misfortune.

"Oh look, cab's here."

Despite being an overnight flight with complimentary wine, Jeff struggled to sleep on the plane while sitting upright. He couldn't sleep anywhere that wasn't his own bed, and he was exhausted from another night of little to no sleep.

Jeff, Randy, and Jim left the airport at Keflavik, and the freezing wind in September made them doubt if this was the right time of year to visit Iceland. Most of their research before the trip had been about Reykjavik, which wasn't far away and presumably the same weather. Their rental car representative desperately tried to hold the door open for them against the prevailing wind.

"It's just windy in this town because we are near the water." The car rental employee reassured them after seeing the concerned look on their faces as they shielded themselves from the gale force winds. "You're going to be fine in other parts of the country this time of year."

"This doesn't seem promising," Jeff replied.

"Trust me. We already have all of your information, so this should be a simple process. You wanted an automatic transmission, correct?"

"We wanted a manual transmission," Jim replied. "We all drive manual cars back at home."

"Oh, sorry about that. We assumed you were from the USA and no one there knows how to drive manual cars."

"We can't escape some stereotypes wherever we go. Automatic is fine."

The three of them tossed their bags in the trunk of the car and they were off toward Reykjavik. Jim offered to drive for the whole trip, it was a sort of meditative activity for him. Randy would take the passenger seat as Jeff thought it was awkward to be in the front with Randy's father. Randy also got car sick whenever he was in the backseat of a car in motion. Jeff was the smallest and youngest of the group, so he was fine with his backseat position in the car hierarchy.

The drive across the Icelandic landscape was like nothing Jeff had ever seen since he'd never left the country besides his cruise. He felt like he was on another planet entirely. Jeff saw all kinds of different colors and tones he didn't know existed on this Earth. The volcanic landscape of fire and ice was like something out of a movie, only possible with a green screen and computer-generated imagery.

Jeff had heard half of the population of Iceland believed in the existence, or at least the possibility, of elves before they left. He was starting to see why. The way the sun was coming in at a weird angle played tricks on his eyes and his mind filled in the gaps of the vast unknown in the middle of this island of Iceland. Random vents of steam rising in the distance appearing like hidden settlements of mythical creatures spread across the landscape. Jeff was starting to think there might be something behind this elf claim.

"The speed limit here is ninety?" Jeff asked his companions.

"That's in kilometers per hour," Jim, a much more experienced traveler, answered.

The fact that Jeff had never left the United States before became apparent. "I don't know what that means. How fast is it?"

"It's right around fifty-five or fifty-six."

"That's much less exciting."

They struggled to find parking once they rolled into town, since they couldn't read the street signs and weren't sure what the parking etiquette and laws were. They found something which felt good enough and were finally at their hostel's restaurant, which served breakfast. The group had some time to kill since they were there before the check in time. The server came over to hand them the menus and they glanced over the succinct sheet of paper.

"What in the heck is up with this menu? We get to choose between either hard-boiled eggs or bread? Where is the breakfast?" Randy asked.

"We don't really do breakfast here like they do in most other countries. I'm assuming you're not from around here?" The server replied as if reading from a script. They were visiting at the tail end of tourist season, so she was probably exhausted from answering the same questions for months and months all summer long.

"We're from the United States. The land of eating a whole pound of bacon for a serving and cinnamon toast crunch crusted French toast."

"You're not going to do that here. The bars in Iceland are open until five a.m. and there's usually a party in the streets with to-go cups after the bars close. Not many people are awake until lunch time rolls around."

"I was getting worried about the food scene, but the nightlife might make up for it." Jeff and Randy looked at each other and gave their silent nod of approval as they always did before they pregamed for a party back home. Drinking alcohol was how they were introduced to each other in the first place and was the glue that held them together.

"Icelanders are super friendly to outsiders. You might even get invited to a house party after the street activity dies down as well. Some people don't want the fun to ever end."

Jeff's mind wandered as he thought about the ulterior motives he usually had when pursuing women after the bars closed. "There was a bit of a hard-boiled egg smell on the way in. Is this place known for their eggs or is something else going on here?"

"It's all the sulfur in the water here. You get used to it."

"It put me in the mood for some hard-boiled eggs. Send some to the table."

They were extremely tired from their overnight flight into Iceland but determined to make the most of their first day in this beautiful country. Driving in a foreign land with barely any sleep didn't seem like the greatest idea. However, they didn't want to waste their time when they were in the land of elves and snow. They embarked on a journey around the south end of the ring road of Iceland on their first day and passed the Hellisheiði Power Station on their way out of town. A geothermal power plant which reminded them of Iceland's commitment to power their entire country with renewable energy in the future, truly inspirational.

The first stop along the way was Geysir which featured geothermal hot springs, boiling mud pits, and geysers which activated like clockwork. Jeff had seen Old Faithful at Yellowstone National Park in the states, but this was intriguing, too. Gullfoss was up next on the itinerary. An incredibly strong waterfall, where approximately 140 cubic meters of water surged down the waterfall every second. It reminded Jeff of the road trip he had taken two years ago to see Niagara Falls. He stayed on the United States side, so this was a much better experience.

Next, the iconic Skógafoss waterfall, which was featured in everyone's social media after they visited Iceland. As they approached the base, Jeff's vision filled with whatever parts of the rainbow he could see as a mist of water sprayed everyone with moisture. Every stream in Iceland is drinkable since they all flow directly from one of the many glaciers in the middle of the island that continuously melts. They filled their bottles and tasted the most delicious water in their lives. Seljalandsfoss was afterward, the waterfall you can walk behind.

After driving for a while, Randy felt the purest water in the world work its way through his system into his bladder. They stopped in the next town, Hella, for a break. Jeff wandered around town and noticed everyone wore the same type of sweater that looked perfect for dealing with the Icelandic winters.

Every store they walked by had some variation of a sign that read "Best Iceland Lopapeysa Here." Jeff realized what he needed to bring back home with him. How jealous would everyone back home be when this world traveler wore his souvenir from the land of fire and ice, keeping him completely warm throughout the approaching winter.

They walked into the next store, realizing they were the only people inside and browsed the clothes. Jeff wanted to ask if the sweaters were itchy and if it needed a layer of clothing underneath. He walked up to the counter to see if there was a bell to ring, only to find a small sticky note that read:

"Working from home today.

Please call or text for service.

Will be there in two min."

Jeff couldn't believe what he saw. Were the people of Iceland this trusting of their fellow citizens, and also the tourists, that they would leave a store completely unattended so anything could get stolen without question? It made Jeff want to trust them in return, and he couldn't fathom anyone would want to steal from such a sweet society. Jeff thought about texting, but he didn't see a sweater design he liked, so they headed out. The prices were too expensive also. Paying almost one hundred dollars for a sweater was out of his budget after seeing the prices of food and beverages on the island. He remembered seeing similar signs out on the main roads of small farms they had passed, so maybe they would find something cheaper outside of a town.

They grabbed a bite to eat before leaving town. The options for lunch were much greater than the mediocre breakfast they had. He couldn't believe there were options on the menu like whale, reindeer, puffin, and even fermented shark. Another group of customers had ordered little sealed mason jars to the table.

"What's in those mason jars you brought to that table over there?" Jeff asked the server as he pointed over to the table that was the center of attention of everyone else in the restaurant.

"It's the fermented shark, an Icelandic tradition. The shark is placed underground for months for it to ferment to be safe to eat. We bring it out in the mason jars, so it doesn't stink up the entire place and scare away customers."

"That just doesn't sound enjoyable. Why do people eat that?"

"It's a display of strength. We request our customers sneak it out of the jar and quickly eat it. We also offer a shot of schnapps to wash it down with, which is surprisingly better tasting than the shark."

After smelling the fermented shark, they ordered the lamb and Atlantic cod for their table to share. The freshness of the food amazed them, nothing like this was available back home.

They kept driving and encountered the otherworldly black sand beaches at Reynisfjara, which were a result of the volcanic activity outside of the town of Vik. The sand was more like rocks and likely wouldn't be a good place to bask in the sun. Jeff wasn't sure if there was sun in Iceland since they hadn't seen it yet. There were great pillars of rock standing ominously out in the water masked by fog that gave Jeff chills.

Finally, their last stop on their travels on this day, Diamond Beach and the glacier lagoon at Jökulsárlón. The eerie stillness and utter silence at the glacier lagoon were unlike anything the travelers had ever experienced before. Even for Jim, who was a well-seasoned traveler and was otherwise bored until now. Jeff had truly felt like he had stumbled onto an exoplanet in an entirely different solar system.

Soon after getting back in their car and driving off, they saw a small farm with an enticing sign and pulled into the driveway.

"Halló." An old woman greeted Jeff as he walked into what appeared to be their home as well as a storefront.

"Hello, we've come to check out your sweaters," Jeff replied.

"Our lopapeysas are made from sheep found right on this land. We don't have a fence, so they aren't actually our sheep. Sheep just kind of roam around the island and stick to particular regions. Iceland is an island, how far can they go?"

"That's interesting. These sweaters must be great. Every local I see has one."

"They are the perfect garment for the weather here in Iceland. They keep you warm in the winter and can also regulate your body to keep you cool if needed, and they also keep you dry in the persistent rain and mist here. They are especially perfect for farmers who need to be warm while they're out working in the cold and maintain a comfortable temperature once their body heat starts to rise from working."

"That is amazing. I need to take one home. This will be perfect for shoveling snow as the winter approaches. I'll take the green one over there, it's my favorite color. I'll take the hat too that matches it," Jeff said as he pulled out his wallet.

"A fine choice." The woman pulled out a handheld credit card machine.

"I did not expect to be able to pay with my credit card here."

"We're pretty far ahead here with technology. You'll see these at most restaurants and they'll bring them right up to the table when you're finished eating."

"We are far behind on some things in the United States."

The five-hour return drive to Reykjavik was arduous, but was worth it after all the astonishing sights they had seen. This was an incredible first day outside of the country for Jeff. There was even a breathtaking aurora borealis display outside of the passenger side window when the night encroached. Jeff wasn't expecting to see anything since the northern light season went from September to March. They had never seen anything so blue and green in the sky which would gyrate and wiggle around so swiftly. Jeff couldn't stop thanking Randy for inviting him along for this journey.

The weary travelers arrived at the hostel in desperate need of a nap after their action-packed day. The place had two bedrooms. One bedroom had a double bed where Jim would stay, and the other bedroom had two twin-sized beds for Randy and Jeff. Their room was on the top floor and had a penthouse feel with tilted walls and ceiling windows on one side. It was small, although it didn't feel that way, as it had a fantastic layout. There was a lot of light and a view of the back garden and the rooftops in front. They found their beds after exploring the place, and the room quickly fell silent.

Randy and Jeff awoke completely refreshed after a brief nap and began discussing the night ahead of them. Driving all day exhausted Jim, but he was still awake after successfully fighting off a nap so he could turn in early and sleep through the night. They heard that alcohol was expensive in Iceland, so they opened the duty-free liquor they bought at the airport on the way there. Since the bars were open until five a.m., they figured people would pregame until around eleven before adventuring out to the bars. Jeff and Randy gathered in the small kitchen.

"To you, Randy. For getting me out of my comfort

zone and inviting me on this trip with your father," Jeff said as he raised his shot glass.

"To me!"

"Skál," Jeff added.

They clinked shot glasses and knocked them back.

"Wait, what did you say?" asked Randy.

"Skál, I figured it was a good idea to look up how to say cheers to people before we got here. I think it means you're taking a drink to your skull or something."

"I like how you operate. Let's not get too crazy tonight though. I don't want to get thrown into a foreign prison and not return home."

"It's weird. I have barely seen any police since I've been here."

"The people are so nice. I can't imagine they have any need for police."

"Apparently, they have a special police unit called 'The Vikings' and they are only needed maybe once a year."

"Let's hope they aren't called tonight."

"Did you know beer was banned in Iceland until 1989?" asked Jeff.

"No way."

"The thought was only the lower-class folks drank beer and banning it would keep them out of trouble. They would instead put a shot of the Icelandic schnapps Brennivín, aka black death, into a lower two percent beer mixture to get drunk instead."

"Where there's a will, there's a way. I suppose."

They showed up at the first bar at eleven and it was

mostly vacant. They thought maybe the internet had deceived them and this wasn't the popular bar they were hoping it was. There was a heavy metal band playing in the basement, and what had the potential to be a lively nightlife environment on the main level.

They tried a couple other places until they decided to grab a drink and settle in with a bar featuring a calm atmosphere. There was a lack of happy hours here that would not afford them the luxury of drinking out on the town without the potential for mischief. They had two drinks and were about to head back to their hostel around midnight when they saw a sea of people heading down toward the main bar area.

"I guess we were just way too early," Randy said as he pointed at the mob of people.

"Let's get weird," Jeff replied.

Randy and Jeff were independent social butterflies after they had some liquid courage from their duty-free spirits. They made friends on their own and introduced each other to different groups of strangers. The bar they landed in became too crowded as the night went on, and they only saw each other in passing at different points in the night to check in.

The bar was so packed, it was impossible to hold a beer without it spilling down the front of their shirts. Despite the exorbitant cost of alcohol, the citizens acted like it was the only thing to do on this island of theirs. A local recommended only drinking shots after replacing Jeff's drink he contributed in spilling. The crowd swayed in unison on the dance floor and chanted to an Icelandic song Jeff had never heard of when a woman in her late thirties locked eyes with him and started to grind on him. They danced for a few songs and exchanged words as much as they could over the loud music until a towering man around her age approached them.

"I've seen you've taken an interest in my wife. She's beautiful, isn't she?"

Jeff was more than a few drinks in at this point after pregaming too early.

"She's gorgeous. I didn't know she was married."

"Well, that isn't an issue here. How would you like to come home with us?"

Jeff had this knack of doing reckless things, especially when drinking, that would provide a cool story after the fact. He remembered the conversation he had earlier in the day with the server about folks from Iceland being friendly and having after parties. Jeff hadn't imagined anything like this. He was never this forward when he was on the hunt after the bars closed.

"Uh, yeah. But I better tell my friend Randy first. We're far from home and he would worry about me if he couldn't find me at the end of the night."

The woman's husband looked around at the over-packed bar. "I don't think you're going to find him in this crowd anytime soon. The only thing he will be worrying about tomorrow is you left us waiting and missed out on the sexual experience of a lifetime."

"That's some sound logic there." Jeff stumbled outside with the couple, followed them to their car, and paused. "You're not going to murder me, right?"

"Icelanders are some of the nicest people in the world, haven't you heard this?" the woman said as she grabbed his hand and pulled Jeff into the back seat with her. Jeff couldn't believe this was happening on the first night. He couldn't believe this woman's husband was in the front seat encouraging her behavior. The woman kissed all over Jeff while her husband drove them home, which didn't seem far.

Jeff waited at their front door on the landing, while the couple shuffled around the house. The woman finally emerged. "Would you like an alcoholic beverage? I know this can be a bit awkward if this is your first time."

"I'm already feeling solid. Why don't we just get into it and see what happens?"

The woman kissed Jeff again as she grabbed his crotch and led him into the bedroom without letting go. She tossed him onto the bed and undressed, throwing clothes seductively in every direction. Jeff was frozen in astonishment until she began helping him with his clothes.

How had he waited this long to start traveling? If it was always like this, then he was going to make traveling his sole purpose in life.

The woman's husband walked in and grabbed a large box of condoms. He tossed one to Jeff. The woman was getting hers on top and Jeff switched positions to take over. He didn't notice the woman's husband had grabbed a hatchet from the same dresser he pulled the condoms from before. Jeff was about to get his when the husband swung the hatchet with lethal force and cleanly sliced through his back between his shoulder blades. He and the woman shrieked but for different reasons. Jeff with terror, the woman with satisfaction. Jeff looked down and noticed red drops pouring onto the woman's exposed chest as the warm liquid flowed around from his back to the front of his body.

Jeff was bathing in his own blood instead of the soothing water of the Blue Lagoon he had planned for that day. The last moment Jeff experienced on this Earth was the woman scooping up his blood with her finger and placing it on her tongue.

Mexico

(November 2017)

Justina lay in her hammock at her apartment in Mérida, thinking about the day she had planned exploring the Yucatan Peninsula. She thought about moving to Mexico for a long time and looked for the perfect area to establish herself. Today, Justina was heading to Campeche to explore the port city's wonderfully preserved baroque architecture and to eat some delicious ceviche. It was hard for her to understand and trust the way ceviche was cooked, fresh raw fish cured in citrus juices, but she couldn't stay away from the delicious taste. Though her stomach growled from the street food she ate from the questionable taco truck the night before, it wasn't going to keep her from the other delicacies of this country.

She wondered why every place she stayed at in Mexico had a hammock. Justina heard it was to keep a person off the floor, where a snake or a scorpion would be able to reach you in the middle of the night. Justina had a hard time sleeping on anything that wasn't a bed, so sleeping in the hammock was certainly not an option. She never saw a snake or a scorpion in Mexico, anyway. Her place had two big rooms with queen beds and two private bathrooms with showers in each. The house had a living room and a kitchen with air conditioning and ceiling fans in all rooms and mosquito nets in all the windows.

She walked out to her rental car and looked back at her cute little yellow one-story house with the flat roof and chuckled when she remembered the checkout instructions. Her host told her to simply toss the keys up on the roof before she left for the airport. She was picturing spare keys accumulating all over the flat roof before the host would do his monthly climb up there to retrieve them.

Justina carried her swimwear whenever she drove out of town in case she stumbled across a hidden cenote she wanted to explore. There were many on the maps with plenty of reviews, however, she wanted to find an undiscovered gem not many other people had been to. Chichén Itzá was an option and was one of the seven wonders of the world, but everyone went there. She had read on some online forums that residents would gather outside of small towns and try to herd tourists to the cenotes existing on their land for a small fee. It would be a much more personalized and intimate experience. It felt like she was supporting a small mom and pop cenote shop who was struggling to stay alive in a sea of other, more well-known establishments.

The drive out to Campeche was gorgeous. Coastal sand dunes featuring wild agave dominating with its rosettes and cacti that looked like giant candles. She wasn't expecting the vast grasslands, shrub lands with tortuous branches, and expansive woodlands as far as the eyes could see. An overwhelming geographical mosaic of green mangroves, bogs, and coastal lagoons scattered throughout.

There were stretches of countryside between small towns where the children would chase her car, wonderstruck by the rare visitor gracing them with her presence. Seeing the town's malnourished dogs was the only downside. Their rib cages on display made her sorrowful, and she wanted to take them all home and make sure they were never hungry again.

Justina thought about how the poor dinosaurs must have felt when the meteor that created the Chicxulub crater north of the Yucatan peninsula caused their extinction. She turned down the music in her car and had a moment of silence for Littlefoot, her favorite Cera, and the whole squad.

Justina was nearing a town when she saw a bunch of small groups of people holding signs. She was still too far away, but she wondered if she would be able to read them when she got closer since they probably weren't in English. She started silently cursing her parents for getting her lessons in Italian instead of Spanish. Justina slowed down as she approached them and couldn't read everything on the signs, but they all had one word in common.

"Cenote aquí!"

"Cenote mas fina."

"El Primero Cenote."

Justina recognized the word they all had in common and realized she was in the middle of a cenote gold mine.

She had her pick of the litter and wanted to make sure she would pick a trustworthy group, since she was traveling alone. Justina also didn't want to pick anyone who gave off a commercial feel. The group of sign holders she would pick would need to be just right. She finally noticed a kid, who appeared to be middle-school aged, riding a bike and waving his arm to follow him. This was the one.

She waved back at him to grab his attention and his face lit up like the Fourth of July. He grabbed his handlebars with both hands and petaled feverishly to lead her to the promised land. Justina followed him for longer than she expected. This must have been an exclusive location. This kid was putting in way more of an effort than everyone else who was trying to draw her in.

She sped up her rental car to pull up beside the child and rolled down her windows.

"Grab on!" she yelled out of her passenger side window.

The child didn't seem to understand. She motioned him to grab onto her side mirror so he could coast along using her car instead of using every bit of strength he had in him to lead her in the right direction. The child latched on and relaxed his legs as they sped along at a reasonable speed which his bike could handle. Justina tried to think of any Spanish she had in her limited language tool belt to connect with the child.

"Muy fuerte!" she yelled as she flexed her left bicep.

The kid didn't seem to acknowledge her broken Spanish, either. She was sure fuerte meant strong in Spanish, as she ordered some fuerte mezcal the previous night and it was fifty percent alcohol. Justina had read there were sixty-nine languages spoken in Mexico, so he must know one of them. Maybe the child only spoke Mayan. She was getting the full Yucatan experience.

The child finally let go and pedaled in front of her for a bit longer; he probably didn't want his parents to see him performing such a dangerous maneuver. He turned into a driveway and Justina parked her car on the opposite side of the road. She looked around to see if this was a decent enough place where she wouldn't get murdered as a solo traveler. There were a couple of other cars which looked like they were also tourists, which was a good sign.

The farm had railroad tracks leading off as far as she could see, with small carts pulled by horses that made it seem like a reasonably legit operation. There weren't many alarms going off here. Another car pulled up a minute later with a couple who obviously looked like they were from the United States, which gave her a few other people to experience this with and to help keep her safe. Strength in numbers, as her mother reminded her before she left home for the trip.

"Hey, how are you both today?" Justina asked the two people as they left their car.

"Not too bad, beautiful day. How about yourself?"

"Can't complain, I stumbled upon this cenote and decided to check it out."

"We had read about this cenote online and had to come check it out."

This cenote apparently wasn't as exclusive as Justina

had thought it was. Regardless, the experience fascinated her so far.

"I'm here by myself, do you mind if I tag along with you two?"

"Perfect, we're always down for a third. Not like *that* though."

Justina and her new friends Corey and Shanisha all gathered their belongings, climbed into the next available cart, and were off to their first cenote. Corey and Shanisha were a married couple from Minnesota and were spending their honeymoon down here in the much warmer weather. The Yucatan Peninsula wasn't exactly where Justina would have picked to have her honeymoon.

The gentleman at the front of the cart leading the horse didn't seem to speak English either. He pointed at the horse. "Rocinante!"

They nodded their heads up and down and smiled as if they knew what he was talking about. *Maybe it was the horse's name?* Before they knew it, they were at their first cenote. Rocinante was an expeditious creature.

They hopped off the cart and stared at the ladder poking out of the giant hole in the ground.

"Do you think this is safe?" Justina inspected the worn wooden ladder which appeared to be built on this farm instead of purchased at a store.

"Ladies first," Corey replied.

Justina was the first to descend into the chasm in the ground, using three points of contact at all times and trembling with each step. The man leading the horse had assured her there was water at the bottom of the hole in the ground. She reached the platform at the end of the descent on the twenty-foot ladder, and it looked as if there was no water at all. She got on her knees and reached her hand down to create ripples in the water to disrupt the sheet of glass she had been previously staring down into to confirm there was water there.

Justina stood up and yelled, "Cannon ball!"

The second cenote Rocinante brought them to, with breakneck speed, was much larger than the first one. There were already other people swimming around, which was much more reassuring. They must have given people more time at this location since they had caught up with another group. There were stairs this time instead of a ladder, so it was more accessible and brighter since the hole in the ground was larger and natural light could enter. The area of the water was about the size of an Olympic swimming pool.

Justina dove off the high platform that would have made any dive instructor mildly satisfied and tweaked her back upon entry. She cautiously swam over to the rope attached at each end which extended across the entire surface of the water. She could feel all the tiny fish nibbling at her skin whenever she was still and decided it was best to keep moving around since she didn't like the sensation. She was treading water and holding onto the rope when she got the terrifying "shark in a swimming pool" feeling as she glanced at the endless abyss of water beneath her feet. Justina knew cenotes were completely enclosed underneath, but who knows what could be lurking in the vast unknown down there? She swam back to the platform like she was going for a new personal record in an Olympic qualifying round.

Justina only dipped her feet in the third cenote, even though it was much shallower and narrower than the other two.

After their fourth ride with old Rocinante, they arrived back at their cars and dried off. She exchanged information with Corey and Shanisha, and Justina made her way to Campeche.

She spent the day in Campeche exploring the walls of the old fort and hoping she would run into the elusive chupacabra during her adventure. Justina wasn't sure if it was the dirty grill that crafted her street meat the night before, or the ceviche she had in Campeche when she got there, but her stomach sent shooting pains in her abdomen. She was not going to let it ruin her plans for the rest of the day, though.

Everyone she passed in town stared at her pale tourist legs. *Were they that blinding when the light hit them?* After starting to pay closer attention, she realized everyone else was wearing pants except for those who were actively engaging in physical activity. Not only that, most of the dogs were even dressed better than her. Many of them had outfits which resembled human clothes, instead of the funny little outfits people make their pets wear on Halloween. It must have been some sort of status thing she was not clued in on. She hadn't packed any pants with her so she was going to have to stick out for the rest of the trip.

Her day would end at the Uxmal Mayan ruins, which

she wanted to see ever since she had climbed Pirámide del Sol in Teotihuacan the previous year when she visited Mexico City. Justina had an obsessive urge to climb to the highest point in Uxmal to get a good view of the area. She needed to post the perfect social media picture that would make everyone back home jealous. Justina entered the Uxmal ruin area and walked right up to the largest temple, a four-sided steep pyramid with holes near the top on two sides. She noticed a small group clapping their hands in front of the temple which created an interesting birdlike acoustic echo when it reverberated from the small cavity in the stairs. To her dismay, there were "No Climbing" signs hung on ropes all around the temple.

Her phone vibrated; it was a text message from Justina's mother:

"Are you still alive?"

"Not only alive, but thriving."

"I need a picture of you, this could be someone else using your phone."

Justina let out an exaggerated sigh at her worrisome mother. She considered taking a selfie, but she wanted to let her mother know all her limbs were still intact and doing perfectly fine.

She approached a random tourist. "Excuse me, could you take a picture of me to send to my mother?"

"Sure."

Justina handed her phone to the other tourist and smiled.

"Wait …"

Justina grabbed a rock to pose with to add some flare

to the photo. She thought about updating her social media followers with a post that said "Rockin' my way through the Yucatan." She had to make sure everyone back home knew she was having a way better time than them and making the most of her vacation.

"Alright, I'm ready," Justina finally said.

"Say Kraft cheese."

Justina sent the picture to her mother and thought how that tourist lady was oddly specific about her cheese. She stalked around the temple, waiting for the coast to clear so she could make her forbidden ascent. She took pictures from every angle to look natural and had probably circled the temple at least three times until the opportunity presented itself.

When she couldn't see anyone from her point of view, Justina sprinted for the temple and climbed like she had never climbed before. The stairs were precipitous and surprisingly well built for how old they were. She finally reached the top and felt a weird sensation she had never experienced before. Justina was awe-stricken by the incredible views that few had been able to experience in recent years. She quickly whipped out her phone and snapped pictures in all directions with the limited time allotted before someone caught her trespassing. Those perfectly framed pictures along with her cenote experience were completely worth the risks she took that day.

Justina looked straight down the stairs after she was satisfied with her pictures, and the feeling she experienced morphed into a dizzying vertigo which threw off her vestibular system. She tried to sit down to situate herself and tripped, and then gravity took its full effect. Justina cartwheeled down the face of the temple, smacking a limb or her own temples on every step, until she reached her final resting area on the ground. She was deceased before she even made it to the ground.

Justina wasn't found until the following morning when a tour guide stumbled upon her and interrupted the iguanas who were investigating her bruised and bloody corpse.

Cuba

(June 2017)

It hasn't always been the case that United States citizens were allowed to travel to Cuba. When the chance presented itself, Adam made sure to hop on the opportunity. Adam wasn't completely sold on the idea of spending an extended period of time there, so he found a cruise which would leave out of Miami and have an overnight docking experience in Cuba. A whole day and night there, followed by half of the next day, would be the perfect amount of time to visit Cuba while it was still available for travel.

Adam had a buddy who had gone to Cuba a few months before. He managed to drag him back down there because Freddy loved to dance and party whenever the opportunity presented itself. Freddy loved a cruise experience and it didn't matter where it was stopping, as long as he got some quality boat time. Adam had heard the Cuban people were insanely friendly and they loved baseball, so he made sure to bring all of his favorite Baltimore Orioles gear to wear around town. The Orioles had been bad for many years, regardless, that was still his team and he wore their shirts and hats anywhere he went.

Adam and Freddy walked down the gangway of the boat enthusiastically, as they knew they didn't have a ton of time in this country before they would have to sail back to Miami. The cruise port was on the eastern edge of Old Havana, near the cobbled square of Plaza San Francisco. They had just gotten through a large building where they needed to hand their paperwork off to Cuban officials to let them know that they were there for "educational" purposes.

"I have a whole itinerary planned for every hour we're here. I trust you too though, since you've been here before," said Adam.

"I probably didn't do everything here since I didn't do any research before the first trip. The only thing I have to do this time is bring back some Cuban cigars for my coworker Al, he won't stop talking about it after I forgot last time."

"I read about this awesome rooftop spot a few blocks away we can start at."

"I know where you're talking about, I'll lead the way."

They walked through the streets and everyone tried to talk to them in Spanish, but the two of them didn't understand a word. Tourists from the United States hadn't been traveling there for long and everyone in town would flock to the cruise port when a boat came in. Many of them tried to sell products or paint pictures so tourists would feel obligated to give them money.

A random person pointed at Adam's hat and yelled,

"Manny Machado!"

"Let's go O's!" Adam yelled back.

"Wow, I didn't know baseball was such a thing down here," Freddy said.

"There are a ton of Cuban players who play professionally, I did my research before I came. I read that a common interest like baseball would go far in overcoming the language barrier."

"I can tell. We're here at my favorite spot from the first trip, is this the spot you were talking about?" Freddy asked.

"It's not. I think it's one more block over."

"Alright, whatever you say. I guess we can see about your research."

They walked another block over to Adam's spot, which happened to be a rundown hotel. It didn't look reputable from the outside and it didn't advertise the fact that there was a rooftop bar.

"I don't know about this, looks a little sketchy," Freddy said.

"Trust me, bro."

They walked into the lobby and approached a worker who was carrying some toiletries from a closet.

"Bar? Drinks?" Adam said, making a motion as if he was knocking back a tasty beverage.

"Cal Ripken." The worker said, pointing at Adam's Orioles hat.

"Si. Cervezas? Donde?"

The worker pointed to the stairs and elevator on the other side of the lobby. The elevator had sliding metal doors attached to it that closed when not in use and there was a staircase which wrapped around the elevator shaft.

"Gracias," Freddy said. He should have paid attention more during Spanish class in high school.

"Let's go," Adam said.

"I'm still having doubts, is that an elevator? It looks like it wasn't built during the last century," Freddy said.

"I guess it's an elevator. I'm definitely not taking that decrepit thing."

"Agreed."

They climbed the six stories of steps taking only one break along the way and walked out onto an incredible rooftop patio with amazing views of the city in all directions. It was one of the tallest viewpoints in town and you could see every building as well as the waterfront where their cruise ship had docked. They were the only people there and had the entire rooftop patio to themselves.

"Dos mojitos, por favor," Adam said to the bartender.

"I can't believe I never found this spot after being here a whole week," Freddy said.

"See, what do you think?" asked Adam.

"I'm thinking I should have done more research before I was here the first time around. We're following your itinerary the rest of the day."

They spent the day bar hopping and seeing all of the views Cuba had to offer. The National Capitol of Cuba had a striking resemblance to the United States White House. They visited Castillo de San Pedro de la Roca and the neoclassical buildings in La Habana Vieja. The two checked out all the bars Ernest Hemingway frequented in the land that invented the mojito and the daiquiri. They saw all the neat old churches and the plethora of vintage cars the Cuban people had amazingly kept running since the fifties.

"Dude, we've done more in one day than I did when I was here for an entire week on the last trip," Freddy said.

"I'm telling you, you need to research places before you go. I have one last trick up my sleeve."

They headed out to the Malecon where everyone went to hang out at the end of the day. A maritime promenade approximately eight kilometers long separated the huge rocks and crashing waves from the wide roadway adjacent to it. The locals head there after work to get the gossip from their neighbors, to try to catch dinner for the night, or to simply drink and have a good time. Even though there was a language barrier between them, the locals took them in as their own. The Cuban people shared their drinks and danced with them while the sun set.

The next day arrived and they were off the boat again for another half a day of enjoying the wonderful island of Cuba.

"The Cuban people are the nicest I have ever met in all of my travels," said Freddy.

"Brooks Robinson!" a stranger yelled as they passed some locals.

"Adam, wearing the baseball gear was such a good move. Everyone was giving us free drinks and being nice to us all based on the shared connection through sports."

"I'm telling you, always research a place before you

go there."

"What does your research say for today?"

"Actually, we did everything on the list yesterday. Do you want to head back to that cool rooftop bar first and take it from there?"

"Sounds like a plan to me."

They walked back to the hotel lobby and stood in front of their choice between the rickety old elevator and the stairs.

"I'm a little hungover," Freddy said. "I think I'm going to take the elevator."

"You're going to trust that ancient thing?" Adam asked.

"I don't trust myself to not puke going up those stairs, I'm going to chance it."

"Alright, we've seen it work a few times. What could go wrong?"

The elevator attendant guided them into the elevator which would fit two additional people if they were slender enough. Adam wondered how anyone would fit in there with their luggage, it was a hotel, after all. Maybe folks sent their luggage up the elevator with an employee and met their luggage at the floor they were staying on.

The employee closed the metal lattice doors that would keep them contained and pressed the button for the rooftop. This was after they had the confusing language barrier conversation and they provided their usual drinking motion sign language. The elevator started to rise and there was a little more of a vibration than they were comfortable with but it was doing its job nevertheless. Adam thought about signing up for Spanish lessons when they got home as they ascended.

"This vibration is not helping my headache," Freddy said.

"You're the one who wanted to take the elevator," Adam replied.

The elevator stopped between the fifth and sixth floors, and the attendant gave them a concerned look. He said a few words in Spanish with a disgruntled tone and reached his arm out of the elevator door opening, signaling to one of the bartenders to assist him. Just as another employee came over to assist, the elevator gave out and dropped half a floor before abruptly coming to a halt. They all caught themselves and the elevator attendant screamed in pain. He turned to Freddy and sprayed him with blood from his nub, where the elevator had completely severed his arm.

Freddy was covered in blood and shrieked at him in horror as if they were having a shouting match to see who could drown out the other's voice. Adam and Freddy backed away from him as if his blood was contagious and would turn them into zombies. They slammed into the opposite wall of the elevator and knocked it loose, causing an ear-piercing whining sound as the elevator fell all the way to the ground floor. The old, rickety elevator had finally had enough and killed all of its occupants after its final descent.

Romania

(August 2016)

The travel crew consisted of six people, which was two people over their usual strict limit of four people they like to travel with. Four was the perfect number for most hotels for sharing beds and rooms. It was a solid number for most train seating arrangements and other public transportation. Gary and Steve had sworn they would never go over traveling with a total of four people ever again after their previous trip, and here they were after being guilted into inviting Josie and Tina along so Amy wouldn't be the only female on their adventure.

Gary, Steve, Josie, Tina, Ryan, and Amy were all doing a huge ten country trip through Eastern Europe. They were trying to knock off as many countries from the goal Gary had of seeing thirty countries before he turned thirty. The group was currently traveling from Belgrade, Serbia to Budapest, Hungary. They decided to stay one night in Timișoara, Romania on the way to add another quick country to the list. Gary and Steve parked their rental cars next to their accommodation and stood outside waiting for their host to let them in.

"Man, I hate it when a place doesn't offer self-check-in," said Gary.

"Yeah, you never know what you're going to get when you meet these people. Are they going to linger and want to hang out with you or simply toss you the keys and get out of your business?" Steve replied.

"What's this guy's name again?"

"Tanner."

"Does that guy over there look like he would be a Tanner?"

Everyone, not so subtly, turned around at the same time to where Gary was pointing. The guy who was apparently not Tanner, despite his similar facial hair choice to their host, looked affronted and shuffled off around the corner.

"So awkward," Gary said. "I guess I should have added a 'don't everyone look at the same time' before that."

"It's fine. We'll never see these people again," Steve said.

Another gentleman walking with passion rounded the corner talking on his phone. He pushed his way through the six travelers and unlocked their door for them.

"I know. I know, I'll take care of it. Bye. I'm hanging up now. Bye. Kisses," the man said as he hung up the phone.

"Hello," Steve said.

"Girlfriends, am I right? I always say, can't live with

them, can't live with them. Am I right? Fellas?"

"Absolutely," Steve awkwardly added.

Tanner showed them around the place without introducing himself or adding any other pleasantries to the conversation; he was a straight shooter. The place had three bedrooms with queen-sized beds in them and a massive living room for them all to hang out in.

"That's everything," Tanner said.

Tanner's phone started ringing. He displayed the screen to Steve and Gary. It read "Property Manager."

"There's *my wife*," Tanner said.

Gary had to walk away to keep from laughing in Tanner's face as he took off answering his phone like Borat.

"Didn't Tanner say he was talking to his girlfriend when he was walking up and he said kisses?" Steve said.

"I couldn't contain my laughter in the situation," Gary replied.

"Then he said his wife was calling afterwards."

"He can't live with them and he has two of them. My man."

The group spent a few minutes inspecting the dodgy apartment which featured a bathtub without a shower head, a bidet, and a fridge with a grotesque odor inside. They were opening every cabinet and closet, as they did in every place they stayed at. This place was surprisingly well stocked.

"Will it do for a night?" asked Steve.

"As long as no one opens up the refrigerator while we're here." Gary had his shirt up over his nose.

"Let's get out of here and head down into town. I really

don't want to drive, though. I would love to have some adult beverages. We could make it another Rakija night."

"It looks like they do have some ridesharing apps here." Gary looked through his phone. "I thought it was public transportation only."

"Sweet. We'll need two of them since there's six of us. Ryan, can you grab the other one?"

"Sure," Ryan said.

"You're not going to believe this. It will be my driver's third trip," said Steve.

"I got you beat. This is my driver's very first ride."

"I don't know how I feel about that. We could just take public transportation," Gary said.

"Stop worrying, it isn't even far. When in Rome, right? We probably won't even get up to forty miles per hour. And look, my guy has a solid four stars," Steve retorted.

"From two reviews. Alright, I want to be in the car with the guy who has at least two rides under his belt."

"Fine."

They were all picked up in front of their apartment a few minutes apart. Steve, Gary, and Josie were with the third-ride driver who arrived first. The others blessed their driver with his first business.

Gary could tell their driver was exuberant about their ride and decided to squeeze in the back with the others so he wouldn't be talking their ears off the entire time. This backfired when the driver kept turning around in his seat for extended periods of time to keep conversation going with them to boost his app rating.

"Hey man, shouldn't you be watching the road a little

more?" Steve asked with an apprehensive tone.

"I apologize. I'm so excited for another ride. Ridesharing apps have recently become available here."

"We can tell."

The driver rummaged around in his glove box at forty-five miles an hour. "Would you all like to see my stamp collection?"

"NO!" Everyone replied in unison.

They were so thankful when they reached their destination in one piece and were practically climbing over each other to get back onto the sidewalk. The first three straightened themselves up on the sidewalk and waited for the other trio before they entered the restaurant. The second car was only supposed to arrive a couple minutes after theirs and five minutes had passed while they were waiting.

"Now we wait for the other group," said Steve.

"What do you think the odds of them making it accident free?" asked Josie.

"Don't joke about that," replied Gary.

"There they are. Not a scratch on their car," Steve said.

The other three jumped out of their car expeditiously, as the first group did.

"No worries, right?" asked Steve.

"Our driver kept turning around in his seat to talk to us and almost mowed over a pedestrian in a crosswalk," exclaimed Ryan.

"Sounds like you all had a similar experience," Gary said.

"All of this fearing for my life has made me hungry."

"Same, I'm starving."

"I'm really hoping they have vegetables here, unlike in Serbia," Ryan said.

"The only choice of having a hamburger with or without cheese was starting to get old."

"Do you think they have vegetables in Rome?"

They went to a small family restaurant in town and were given the biggest table inside. The group had the place to themselves. Gary had been worried the entire trip about ordering off menus in different languages. The server going around the table reminded him of waiting his turn to read a paragraph in front of his middle school class and fumbling over the words in front of everyone. Gary got another hamburger, as he had been doing in Serbia the previous two days. Steve ordered a branzino and was caught off guard when they brought the entire fish, scales and all. The fish was still staring at him with its intact eyes for the entire meal. He acted like he knew what he was doing but barely picked at it despite talking about how hungry he was all day.

The crew was at the restaurant for a prolonged time. They had thought being the only people in the restaurant would speed things up a bit, however, no one was in a rush to take care of them. It was strange and felt rude to have to flag someone down for the check to pay. The server assured them it was normal to do so in most of Europe. They had plenty of time to discuss the rest of their trip ahead of them, which would end with driving through Switzerland and turning in their rental cars in Milan, Italy.

They took public transportation back to the apartment.

Switzerland

(August 2016)

Sixty percent of Switzerland is made up of the alps, however, Switzerland can only claim fifteen percent of the alps as their own. The highest and most extensive mountain range in Europe is shared with France, Italy, Liechtenstein, Austria, Germany, and Slovenia. The Swiss Alps feature some of the most scenic areas in all of Europe, which also cause some of the most dangerous driving situations in the world. There are many mountain passes which close for most of the winter due to the fact that snow and ice can make them literal death traps. It was cold enough for snow at the top of the mountain passes to cause a closure in August. The fact that they were deemed safe for car traffic at this time did not make them completely free from risk.

The six travelers, led by Steve and Gary, were far from Romania and in their ninth country of their extended odyssey through Europe. In this scenario, the amount of people they were traveling with was the cause for them to need two cars in this precarious situation. Steve was a seasoned manual transmission driver and also an international driver's permit holder. Gary, not so much. He had owned a manual transmission automobile a few years ago, so Gary was not completely unfamiliar with the concept. It wasn't fresh in his mind, either. Regardless, he had agreed to be the other person to get an international driver's permit, as long as he could follow Steve's car wherever they went. Steve had a tendency to drive fast and not always wait for Gary.

They had only spent a couple of hours grabbing a bite to eat in the city of Vaduz in Liechtenstein, which offered the chance to add another quick country to their count. Gary couldn't stop thinking about the unexpected squat toilet they encountered there; he was so glad he only had to pee during the stop. That quick meal had cost them a front passenger side tire as Gary got a flat immediately after leaving Liechtenstein. Steve decided not to wait for Gary and kept on driving without him.

Gary's passengers did not offer to help him change the spare tire and after their second auto shop stop, they found a person who spoke decent English and had the tire replacement they needed. Both front tires needed to be replaced for the car to drive correctly and they were hoping their travel insurance covered it. Gary had caught up to Steve again, who finally waited for him at a gas station.

"We could either take a train where we drive our cars right into it that travels right through the mountain for a fee, or we could drive the mountain pass that is still open this time of year," said Steve.

"I haven't stalled my car out yet and I'd rather not press my luck up some insanely steep roads," replied Gary.

"Did I mention it's free?"

"You can't take those extra euros with you when you're six feet under, Steve."

"Well, this mountain pass was featured in my favorite James Bond movie of all time, so we're driving it whether you want to or not."

"The illusion of choice. You're going to be the death of me," Gary said as he shook his head and rolled his eyes.

"You've come all this way. You wouldn't want to miss out. When in Rome, right?"

They had been saying the phrase the entire trip, despite the fact that they weren't even visiting Rome. Their trip did end in Italy. However, the last and only city in Italy they were visiting was Milan, not Rome.

"Fine, but you better drive slow," Gary said.

They set off along the straightaway which went from the current gas station and approached the mountain head-on. This road led up the back-and-forth sections connected by hairpin turns that weaved their way up the mountain. Steve had his windows rolled down, blasting techno music like he was trying to creep down the avenue back home and impress all the girls with his new sound system. This car did not have an impressive stereo system, though.

Gary had turned down the volume all the way in his car to see better, naturally. Josie was in the passenger seat of Gary's car acting as his copilot, calling out the turns ahead in detail as they came up on her phone GPS to make Gary feel better. This mountain was a team effort. Except for Tina, who was in the back of Gary's car sipping on the emotional support schnapps in the backseat to forget about her fear of heights.

It took fifteen minutes of back-and-forth driving to get to the hotel rest area most of the way up the mountain. Turning left, going straight, turning right, going straight. Over and over again. Gary couldn't get the car out of second gear and had to switch to first gear a couple of times, even though they never stopped on their way up, to get the struggling rental car to overcome the forces of gravity on these steep inclines.

They parked at the rest area by the hotel near the top of the mountain and looked over the gorgeous landscapes they previously came from. They could only see a few sections of the winding road they had ascended because it was so steep. Rolling green hills, snowcapped mountains, and clouds as far as they could see in every direction. The only sign of civilization was the tiny flat road hundreds of feet downward that brought them there. They were on top of the world. Even Tina got out and took notice of the terrifyingly beautiful heights, staying away from the edge of the cliffs, of course.

"Ready to head down the other side, Gary?" asked Steve.

"I guess so," Gary reluctantly replied.

"C'mon, the upside is the easiest part. All of the clutch work is over. Now we cautiously drift back down."

"Let's get this over with."

It turned out the hard part was not over with. The way back down was ten times worse than the way up. Gary regretted his decision to be the other international drivers permit holder and also for inviting too many people on this trip to necessitate two cars.

Gary looked up the entire time they were ascending the mountain. If he were looking down behind him at all, he would have realized none of the straightaways had barriers, and they were straight drop-offs hundreds of feet down. Now, they had to stare at their death below the entire way down the other side of the mountain. Gary thought the turns would be the worst part, but at least there was a small guardrail, unlike the straight sections, that might keep them from tumbling to their doom.

"Josie, why aren't you helping call out the turns ahead like before?"

Gary quickly glanced over at Josie on one of the straightaways instead of looking off of the cliff. Josie was holding the overhead handle and the dashboard with her completely white knuckles. Her phone had slid from her lap onto the carpet a long time ago. It didn't look like she was taking her eyes off of the road anytime soon to retrieve her phone to start calling out the turns to help Gary.

"Josie?" Gary asked again.

Gary couldn't hear anything over Tina screaming in the back of the car. He still had the music turned down so he could see better. There was no volume button on the shrieks of terror that exceeded the abilities of their speakers erupting from the back seat of the car.

"You're definitely not helping, Tina," Gary yelled at

her to try and snap her out of her fear.

Gary had the car shift knob in the first gear position, although he never engaged the gear as he drifted as slow as he could, never completely letting off of the brakes all the way down the mountain. The smell of brake pads failing had completely filled the car and overpowered the smell of spilled schnapps previously occupying it. They weren't even halfway down the mountain at this point.

"Josie, I'd really appreciate your help," Gary pleaded with Josie when there was a break in Tina's overture of screams.

A local motorcyclist had sped past them on one of the straightaways like they were holding up a long line of traffic. Tina was still screaming in the back of the car in between taking large gulps of schnapps to calm her nerves. Gary's left foot was still pressed on the clutch, with his right foot visibly quivering over the brake and engaging it every few seconds.

"You're still not helping, Tina."

After ten minutes of absolute terror, they had made it to the final straightaway that led them away from the mountain. Steve decided to pull off on the side of the road to give their legs a short break from the clutch and brake ballet they had just performed.

"Dude," was the only thing Steve could say.

"I hate you," Gary protested as he shoved him into the grass.

Tina was outside of the car, dry heaving. Josie, a germaphobe, was kissing the ground next to the car. Steve's passengers were embracing each other like they thought it would be the last time they would ever get the chance again.

"Did you die though?" asked Steve.

A couple hours of normal driving had passed and the travel crew was finally halfway in between Liechtenstein and Milan. They had picked out a nice little hiking excursion to break up the monotony of driving and to release some of the tension from the terror they had endured. They parked at the base of the mountain in the parking lot where the gondola took passengers up to the top. The group was determined to not take the gondola and earn the views at the lake on top of the mountain which resulted from the hike. They were all in the parking lot staring up at the peak of the mountain where a few boulders had broken loose, causing a tiny landslide.

"There's a mountain here. Do you think we can drive up and down it?" asked Steve.

Gary gritted his teeth and shook his head. "Too soon, man."

"Last one to the top is a rotten egg."

The crew had only been hiking for ten minutes up the mountain and had already taken a few breaks for various reasons. Tina had not quit smoking as she had promised in her new year's resolution and her lungs were making her aware of that failure. Steve had sworn up and down he was going to get back into running this year. He had never managed to get outside and work towards his goal more than twice that year. At least the scenery was nice to look at while they were taking a break. They were in the middle of a massive valley with pine trees covering the mountains on either side. There was a river flowing back and forth down the valley they were crossing over on bridges as they made their way up the trail.

Gary was doing fine physically and thinking about their hotel situation when they would get to their destination, while the others were most likely thinking about somehow surviving the hike. The room had two bunk beds against one wall and a queen-sized bed on the opposite side of the room with a desk next to it. There were two rooms attached to their one large bedroom. One room had a toilet with a sink. The other had a shower stall and a sink. There was also a public bathroom on the second floor of the building that would most likely get used for handling their morning business. Six people basking in a single room with all their body odor and farts was already enough.

Two of the ladies would take the queen-sized bed so the guys wouldn't have to build the old pillow barrier between them at night. Gary would have to take one of the upper bunk beds since he was the smallest and most athletic out of the group. You can take everything you want up to a top bunk bed, but once you were up there, you always seemed to forget something and would need to climb back down or ask for assistance. Going to the bathroom at night would prove to be an absolute hazard like the situation they had recently survived. Gary was looking around at his out of breath companions, dreading the upcoming sleeping arrangements.

"We're never going to make it up this hill if we have

to keep stopping every few minutes for you sloths," Gary said.

"Not everyone is a star athlete and free from vices like you, Gary," Steve replied.

"Don't get snippy with me after what you put me through today."

"There's a gondola that will take us to the top for a small fee."

"So now you're alright with a small fee as long as it means you don't have to be healthy and in shape."

"Whatever, you can join me if you want. Up to you. Anyone else with me?"

Everyone besides Gary was in agreement about taking the gondola so they could make it before sunset and enjoy the views at the lake at the top.

"Fine, we can all take the lazy way up there," Gary conceded.

They hiked down to the gondola launch center and paid ten euros each for a single day pass. Their group of six, instead of their usual four, had betrayed them again as they all could not fit on a single gondola with the people who were already ahead of them. Steve and the two passengers from his car went ahead as they had been doing all day in their two-car fleet.

A minute passed as Gary, Josie, and Tina waited for another gondola car to come around. They all climbed aboard with some other folks who were waiting in line and departed from the gondola launch center while Tina squeezed Josie's thigh with a vicelike grip. The gondola cart bobbed up and down as they ascended and it offered incredible views of the surrounding valleys and mountain peaks. They could see their rental cars in the parking lot getting tinier as they got farther away.

Tina was just starting to ease her grip when they heard a loud cable snapping sound coming from higher up and ahead of them. Their gondola cart started plummeting to the ground as everyone inside left their seats that gravity was previously keeping them attached to. The cart fell fifteen meters and landed on a flat spot on the mountain as the passengers were abruptly returned to their seats and the ground of the cart with near lethal force. Bodies were strewn throughout the cart in all different varieties as the group began to assess their collective injuries. Everyone seemed to have survived, although no one was completely unscathed and a few passengers had suffered serious injuries. Landing on a flat spot of the mountain incline and resting in place had saved them.

They heard a crunching metal sound as they turned their attention up the mountain to see the source of the sound was the gondola cart containing their three other friends. Gary had been following Steve in their cars all day, but now Steve was careening down like a boulder in pursuit of Gary. The passengers able to move screamed and pulled at the door of the gondola containing them. It was stuck from the impact of falling and wasn't budging. The gondola that had departed before them collided with theirs like two croquet balls and sent them tumbling end over end from their flat area where they were resting. Bodies were sent frantically from wall to wall of the gondola the rest of the way down the mountain, like coins inside of a child's piggybank as it was shaken to figure out how much money was inside.

The final descent would prove fatal for everyone inside of both of the gondolas that had just departed the launch center. Their two rental cars would sit in the parking lot for an entire month before they were finally picked up to be cleaned out and rented again.

Colombia

(January 2019)

"I have to admit, Mindy, when you told me your son moved to Colombia to enter the coffee industry, I thought for sure he was manufacturing cocaine." Blake was sitting in his cubicle when his coworker stopped by and leaned over the small divider surrounding his desk.

"What did you think I was doing down there when I went to visit him? I even brought you back some of the coffee his company produced," Mindy replied.

"I watched your cat for the week because you're my favorite coworker. I was also afraid I was becoming some kind of accomplice to a crime family."

"Come on, how long have you known me?"

"Both of those products came from the same plant, right?"

"You're also a world traveler. Why don't you go down there for yourself and check out his operations?"

"I've always been more of a European traveler. I guess it could be time to knock another continent off of my list."

"You'll even have Daniel down there to give you the

true local experience."

Blake hung out with Mindy's son, Daniel, a couple of times before he left for Colombia since they were the same age.

"Why not, let me ask a couple of friends and see if they're interested in coming with me."

"I'll tell Daniel to take care of you just like he did with me. It's a beautiful country, you'll see."

Blake and his best friend, Will, decided it was time for a change from their usual Europe backpacking experience. They took Mindy up on their offer to visit her son Daniel. The two seasoned travelers headed down to Medellín with their limited knowledge of Spanish and their slight fear of the crime Colombia had a reputation for.

There are two large mountainous regions that make up the Aburrá Valley that surrounds the city of Medellín. This valley provides a stable climate that gives Medellin the nickname of the "City of Eternal Spring." The weather was perfect as they drove into town from the airport and their taxi driver even pulled over at a couple of different lookouts on the mountainside on the way into the city to take in the view. Rows and rows of houses went almost entirely up the mountains on each side and was a sight they had never seen before.

They had rented a six-bedroom accommodation because it wasn't much more expensive than anything else available, so they thought why not live it up. The pictures online were deceiving in a lot of places they looked at so they went for it. Their place had six bedrooms as promised and all of them included full-sized beds. The bathrooms were outside; there were three separate shower stalls and three separate bathroom stalls. It appeared to have been a hostel with shared facilities in a previous life but was now rented out as a whole. It was anomalous for those two to be there with the abundance of bedrooms and facilities.

On the first full day of their vacation, they did a free walking tour. The tour guide warned them of pickpockets and told them to keep their backpacks in front of them at all times and their belongings in their front pockets. The two felt safer there than they had on many of their trips in Europe. There were less people around that they needed to keep their eyes on and the streets were cleaner than most places they had been to before. Blake and Will were having a side conversation while they received the safety briefing they had heard on all of their other free walking tours.

"I have to say, this place doesn't have the best reputation. However, I feel way safer than I do back home in Chicago," said Blake.

"Right, this place is much cleaner too." Will looked around the clean sidewalks and streets.

"It seems like the people are all genuinely interested in us and want to welcome us to the city."

The tour guide ended the usual initial walking tour introduction. "Again, I'm Paul. Let's head to our first location."

Blake and Will were at the front of the group and had a side conversation with Paul as they walked.

"Everyone warned us not to come here. This place seems super safe though. What's that about?" Blake asked.

"The city has been very safe for decades now and we can't seem to shake the reputation on the international front. There are still some kidnappings that happen out in the countryside, but the cities are completely safe," Paul answered.

"Kidnappings you say?"

"Yes, it's mostly people who are related to rich families in the area and the occasional tourist who gets lured in as a bribery sort of situation. It's rare, though. It's still something we like to warn people about so they can keep their wits about them while they're visiting. We don't want more unfortunate stories to come from our beautiful country."

"Like some sort of coffee business scheme or something?"

"Huh?"

"What?"

"Alright," Paul said to the group. "We're at our first stop on the tour."

Blake didn't listen to anything the tour guide said for the rest of the time they walked around the beautiful city. He thought he had heard something about how much their rail system was their greatest pride, regardless, he could only think about what Paul had said in the beginning about kidnappings. There's no way Mindy could have set them up. They had been coworkers for years. Blake was even her go-to cat sitter. Who would watch Tinkerbell if he got kidnapped or murdered in Colombia?

The tour concluded and Blake and Will headed to the

coffee shop they were supposed to meet Daniel at, but they were having second thoughts.

"Are we going to talk about what Paul said about the kidnappings here?" Will asked.

"Yes, I couldn't hear anything else he said the entire tour," Blake said.

"Me neither! I know he kept talking about public transportation. What are we going to do? There's no way we can still meet up with this guy."

"We'll feel it out, and we'll head back early tonight, alright?"

"Alright, fine."

They walked into the coffee shop and Blake tried to remember what Daniel looked like when he met him three years ago. Daniel noticed the two Americans who stuck out like a sore thumb and approached them.

"Welcome to Medellin! How was the walking tour?" Daniel asked.

"Definitely informative. We learned a lot about history and crime and whatnot. The part about the crime was interesting," Will replied sarcastically.

"I was concerned when I first moved here, but there is absolutely nothing to worry about. Let's get out of here. Are you all hungry? There is this perfect restaurant in town that puts this red wine crust on the steak. It's to die for."

"I'd rather not die today," Will said.

Blake punched Will in the arm.

Daniel gave them a weird glance. "I have a coworker and his wife meeting us there too. The people here love taking care of tourists."

They went to the restaurant and ate the most perfect steak they had ever had in their life, and for half the price of anywhere back home in Chicago. Daniel introduced them to aguardiente, which is a deceptively strong alcoholic beverage the locals refer to as "fire water." They drank and drank despite their gracious host telling them they wouldn't party too hard while having work in the morning. They finally decided to call it a night and stood out front of the bar.

"So, Colombia hasn't caught on with the ridesharing apps yet. It's actually illegal here," Daniel said. "I'll call you one and one of you will have to sit in the front seat. It makes it less suspicious."

"That works, I wouldn't want either me or a local driver trying to make a living to be thrown in jail tonight," Blake replied.

The car pulled up and Daniel confirmed it was the correct driver. Blake got in the passenger seat and Will sat in the back.

"How's your night going so far? A lot of business?" Blake asked their driver.

"No hablo inglés."

"Sorry. Um. Lo siento."

They were halfway through their silent car ride home when Blake replayed the conversation they had with their tour guide, Paul, from earlier in the day. He sobered up instantly when he thought about the possibility of being kidnapped for ransom and never returning back to Chicago. Blake and Will had no involvement with requesting and confirming the identity of their driver that had picked them up. Blake was terror stricken as he thought about his options.

"Hey, we're pretty close to our place. You can just let us out here," Blake nervously said.

"Que?"

"Please, let us out and don't murder us!"

The driver was caught off guard by his sudden desperation, but still wasn't completely sure of what he was asking.

"Please, I'm begging you, let us out here," Blake said as he pointed at the sidewalk.

Blake looked back at Will, who looked like he was about to start strangling their driver to get out ahead of the situation.

"Aquí?"

"Yes, please!"

"Claro."

The driver pulled over as Blake and Will were practically tucking and rolling out of the car that had not come to a full stop yet.

"Adios!" the driver called out with a perplexed look on his face.

Blake and Will were silent as they sprinted back to their six-bedroom accommodation and slammed the door closed behind them. They slept in two bedrooms close to each other that night in case there were some sort of intrusion and they needed strength in numbers. They were completely paranoid as they awoke at every little sound and didn't get much sleep.

***

Blake and Will walked up to the base of Guatapé the next day. Guatapé is a 675 feet tall rock that requires ascending 649 steps to see the breathtaking views of the surrounding landscape.

"We are still in agreement. He was thinking about kidnapping us and we spooked him out when we started acting funny right?" Blake asked. They hadn't talked about it much the night before as they were too traumatized from the experience immediately afterward. Blake was finally ready to level set to see if they were on the same page.

"Totally, after we took the element of surprise away, he changed his mind about the whole operation," Will said.

"What is my coworker going to say when I tell her about what happencd?"

"I wouldn't say a word. You might not be able to say a word to her ever again if we die trying to climb these steps."

"My head is bumping from all the fire water. There's no way I'm missing out on these views, though."

"The stairs are the only way up?"

"Yes, are you ready to start?"

"No, I'm just going to stay down here."

"What? You came all this way and you're not going to check this out?"

"Nope, send me pictures at the top though."

Blake began his ascent. He had always heard the best way to get over a hangover was to sweat it out through exercise. Those were his thoughts as he completed the first flight of stairs. *Only a million more to go*. His headache was taking full effect already. He had to power through it and sweat out the alcohol.

He thought about all of his half marathons he ran back home and how this was nothing compared to that. Two more flights of steps had him reconsidering. Are steps much different from running in Chicago? It's not exactly flat there either. Is the elevation different in Colombia? The headache wasn't getting much better after a few more flights of stairs.

Blake thought about all those nights where he drunkenly walked home from the bar. A couple of times he ended up walking five or six miles back home from the bar with the old booze brain thinking it was a solid plan. His drunken mind probably thought he needed to do some extra last-minute training for his next race and figured what better time than the present? He felt his heartbeat through his entire body now.

He had to be getting close to the top. He thought about all the mental gymnastics he would perform while running. Blake would run faster on the uphill sections during a race to get them over with faster, instead of the usual reaction where everyone would slow down for hills. He couldn't stop and take a break here either, he would only see how much further it was and might give up. He felt like he was dying but the symptoms would subside soon enough when he got to the top and saw the amazing views.

He couldn't think about anything in life anymore besides the next step of his climb. Left foot. Right foot. Left foot. His heart was beating multiple times between each of his steps, and he timed each heartbeat to the rhythm of his next step. He was so focused on each step and the views at the top that he completely disregarded the angina which crept in on the last staircase. He clawed at his own chest as if something was trapped inside and went into cardiac arrest at the top of the last step.

There wasn't anyone at the top who knew CPR and no way to get assistance in the time it would take to save Blake's life.

Sweden

(December 2018)

Sarah and her boyfriend Chris were in their last destination of their four-country Northern European trip, Sweden. Sarah didn't have much interest in visiting the country, but it was the cheapest place to fly home from. Chris, however, had heard of the tale of the Gävle Goat, and knew seeing it must be a part of their trip if they were in this part of the world in December.

The Gävle Goat is a traditional Christmas display set up on the first day of Advent every year and stands in Slottstorget (Castle Square) for all to revel at. The forty-two-foot-tall goat is constructed with hay and rope and usually takes a couple of days to construct. It's displayed for as long as it survives.

There's a fun tradition where people like to destroy the goat, and they have done so thirty-seven out of the previous fifty-two times up until 2018. The goat has mostly fallen victim to arson or other forms of vandalism over the years. Everyone always comes up with new ways to bring about the goat's ultimate demise. Security detail and continuous monitoring of the goat have been implemented over the years, but the people always find a way around those measures to ensure chaos.

Chris was obsessed with this tradition and needed to see this goat with his own eyes. The loving couple waited for a taxi at the airport to take them to their accommodations.

"Every year you promise me a beach vacation where I can just lay out in the sun and read, and every year you bring me out on these cold multicountry trips that are way too fast-paced. If it weren't for the years I've spent in this relationship, I wouldn't have come at all," Sarah said.

"Next year, I promise."

"Here we go again. You're all promises and no delivery. Like the ring you've been promising me. What am I going to tell all my friends when I tell them you didn't propose to me in our glass igloo in Norway under the aurora borealis?"

"You're more worried about the social media post for the engagement and the likes than you are about me popping the question."

"I don't even know if I would say yes at this point."

"It would save me a lot of money."

"It's always about money. You're always planning these budget trips where we're staying in hostel twin beds and not alone with each other."

"I'm finally getting some good sleep, at least."

"And you'll continue to get good sleep when you're sleeping on the couch back home. And you'll continue to be celibate like we have this entire trip."

"I guess this is our taxi."

"We will continue this conversation when we get to the place. We are not doing this in front of our taxi driver. Enough people have probably overheard us here already."

"Looking forward to our conversation once we get there."

Sarah and Chris climbed in their taxi and didn't bother speaking with their driver, who appeared to be fine with that. He could probably see the contempt in their eyes and didn't want to stoke the flames anymore. Sarah was starting to become very jealous of her single friend Bridget, who had just ended her relationship and was jetting off to explore Australia. She wouldn't have to share a bathroom with anyone else or put up with snoring for her entire trip.

There was a traditional Christmas market across the beautiful square Stortorget when they arrived. Many different Swedish Christmas sweets and other seasonal delicacies were served alongside various craft items, from iron works to ceramics. Light snow on the buildings and stands added to the romantic atmosphere and glögg, the Swedish version of mulled wine, would help get anyone into the holiday spirit.

"I'm not sure if my liver can handle drinking anymore, although it helps with dealing with you," Chris said.

"We have to try a tunnbrödsrulle, and I don't want to have one sober," replied Sarah. She may not have been interested in Sweden, but as a foodie, she did research the food of each country she visited.

"What in the world is that word you said?"

"A tunnbrödsrulle?"

"It's a drunken delicacy," the driver said. "Mashed potatoes, sausage or hot dogs, lettuce, shrimp salad, mayonnaise dressing, onions, ketchup and mustard, and served wrapped up in a tortilla or flatbread."

"I think I'm going to need to have about twelve beers for that to be something which goes anywhere near my mouth," Chris said.

"I am certainly not going anywhere near your mouth," Sarah retorted. "Let's get some normal people's food first."

"I would be reminisced if I didn't grab some meatballs from an IKEA before I leave this city."

"You're such a child. Also, I think the word you were looking for was remiss."

"I see IKEA Kök right around the corner from our place on the map, which loosely translates to, IKEA kitchen. Let's go!"

The weary couple were on day nineteen lugging their heavy backpacks around. Chris had a new pep in his step as they rounded the corner to meatball heaven. After taking pictures out in front of the store for all of their social media followers back home, they waltzed through the front doors as if they were discovering a hidden chamber of a forbidden temple. There were cabinets and kitchen counters and appliances as far as the eye could see.

"Hallå!" an employee at the front door said.

They didn't exactly look Swedish, but close enough to be mistaken for locals.

"What is this place?" Sarah asked the employee.

"Ah, out of towners." The store employee switched to

his English accent. "This is a kitchen remodeling store."

"Where are the meatballs?" Chris asked.

"This is the fifth time this month. We have a strict no meatball policy here. This is the place you go to before the meatballs can be made."

The two walked out of the store disappointed, famished, and argumentative.

"Did you even look at the pictures online?" asked Sarah.

"No, I didn't look at the pictures," Chris said dejectedly.

"You could have easily seen it was a remodeling store and not a place that serves food. You're such an idiot."

"I know, dear," Chris replied.

"I'm going to look up a place to eat since you can't even handle a task as simple as food."

The two had their spats all trip long and lately it was starting to occur more frequently over the smallest inconveniences. They ended up eating at a fast-food restaurant which they could have eaten in any part of the world. Chris and Sarah wanted to end the argument and start to work on regaining the flame they had remembered from the earlier days in their relationship.

They were back in their last budget hostel for the trip. They had a top and lower bunk across from another bunk bed setup with four lockers in the corner that were assigned to each individual bunk. Chris and Sarah were given bedsheets at the front desk and had to put them on the bed themselves. The window offered a bleak look out into the small courtyard where you could only look into other people's rooms.

"You said you wanted more alone time. How about you go see this stupid goat by yourself?" Sarah asked.

"You know you have some interest in seeing it."

"Not with you, I don't."

"Come on, you're halfway across the world. You will regret it once you're back home and I'm telling everyone the tale of the goat and how we almost took it down, except our attempt was thwarted by the authorities at the last second."

"As long as you promise not to talk the entire way there and the entire way back."

"No deal. We need to scheme about how we're going to make our attack."

Sarah stared at Chris derisively.

"Alright, no talking on the way there or back."

"Alright, I'll come."

"Put your shoes on."

"Wait, did you go sock-shoe-sock-shoe like an absolute psychopath?"

"What do you mean?"

"Everyone else in the world does it sock-sock-shoe-shoe, how have I not noticed this after all these years?"

"Put your shoes on however you prefer and we'll go pick up our rental car."

The adoring couple finally got to the goat after a couple of hours of driving in silence, besides when Sarah was yelling at Chris for his driving style. Chris admired the goat with the same eyes he had for Sarah when they met on their university campus so many years ago. Sarah even brightened up as she found the perfect angle with the exact lighting that would highlight her good side for a photo opportunity.

"Here we go again, always with the photos first. Why can't you live in the moment for once?" Chris asked.

"Maybe I wouldn't have to take pictures of my feet and sell them online if you wouldn't be spending all our money on dumb excursions like this all the time."

"I can't wait for our kids to grow up and find all of their mother's feet photos spread all over the internet."

The two were so busy arguing with each other they didn't notice the next sabotage of the Gävle Goat happening right in front of them. There was a blue sedan careening down the road pointed right at the goat, which hoped to survive for a second year in a row. The determined driver was aiming his car exactly where he would be able to take out the goat's legs and speed off to tell the tale and hopefully not get arrested.

A patch of black ice would result in the universe having a different plan for the goat.

The driver swerved left, then overcompensated right, and crashed into the two travelers. Guts and blood sprayed over the car and the building they were pinned against. They had taken the goat's place in the assassination attempt that could have potentially been avoided if they were paying attention and not screaming at each other.

The Gävle Goat would go on to survive that year with only minimal damages from an attempted arson, resulting in a damaged left front leg. The same cannot be said about the two travelers.

Canada

(July 2022)

Tim was three hours into their nine hour drive to Quebec City from Philadelphia, Pennsylvania. Jeremy was sound asleep in the passenger seat, and Devin was snoring away in the back seat next to the cooler filled with frosty beverages. Tim worked for a utility company and had been on storm duty night shift the week before the trip, so he offered to drive the others through the night to avoid traffic. It would only be another three hours before they got to the border and another three hours until they reached their destination. Then they could eat all the poutine they could get their hands on.

Tim had his "Not So Guilty Pleasures" playlist going for most of the trip but turned on the music he liked since the others were asleep. Experimental progressive metal was more of his taste. It would keep him awake through the long hours in the night, as it did when he drove around for work assessing storm damage the week before.

The border was there before Tim knew it, as he grooved to the polyrhythmic section of a song his second favorite band had recently released. He turned down the music and yelled at his friends to wake up to meet the border crossing agent with him. They pulled up to the empty border station since they drove at such a weird hour of the night. The border agent spoke to them in French like they were residents of Canada.

Tim was not expecting the French and greeted the agent with a weird European accent that didn't seem to have a particular origin which sprung from his sleep deprived mind, "Hallo!"

"Oh, hi. Passports, please." The border agent was caught off guard by his fabricated accent.

Tim handed over the passports, opened to the passport picture and stacked in a neat pile. He was a thorough planner and didn't want any trouble at the border. Tim was worried they wouldn't let him in due to his DUI. He had read they don't let people into Canada with those sorts of credentials.

"Thanks. How many days will you be in Canada?" the agent asked.

"Three days."

Tim was briefed to answer the questions exactly as they were asked and to not provide any additional information that would give off the impression they were nervous and had something to hide. They had absolutely nothing to hide. Either way, they didn't want to waste time being searched at the border.

"Where are you heading?"

Tim was expecting an "eh" after every statement and question. That was just something he had seen in cartoons before.

"We're heading up to Les Escoumins for whale watching. I hope I said it correctly."

"You didn't, but that's alright. French isn't the easiest language to learn. You have to keep your mouth tight to make the sounds right. Did you all book a large boat or a smaller one."

"Um." Tim wasn't expecting her to be so chatty and interested in their whale watching experience, he looked at Jeremy and hoped he would save him. He had been briefed on some of the questions the border agent might ask, however, Tim didn't have much of a hand in planning the trip.

"We're going out on a ten-passenger boat," Jeremy said from the passenger seat.

Tim didn't know the boat they planned to see the massive whales would be such a tiny one. A vessel that small seemed like it could be easily capsized or swallowed whole by a whale if given the opportunity.

"Perfect, that's the best way to do it. You're all set to go. Have a wonderful time in Canada."

Tim grabbed the passports from the agent, rolled up the window, and pulled away from the guard shack.

"That was a lot easier than I expected. She was so friendly," Tim said.

"No passport stamps though. I was hoping to get a stamp," Devin said from the back seat as he inspected his passport.

They drove for another couple of hours as Tim switched over to his "No Foolin, Straight Coolin" playlist which was an obvious crowd pleaser. He adjusted to the kilometers per hour instead of the miles per hour signs Tim was used to south of this border. Americans will use anything to measure besides the metric system. It was at that point he realized they were only three American football fields from their hotel.

They explored the town and ate poutine until they couldn't handle any more delicious French fries and gravy and cheese curds. Tim tried to keep up with the others despite being awake for over twenty-four hours. Although Tim was delirious now, they pressed onward and ended up at a bar where they played heavy metal music. Jeremy hated this music, but he picked it because it would most likely raise Tim's morale and keep him out as late as he wanted to stay out.

They met a lovely young lady wearing all black who seemed like she was trying to seduce them. She mentioned she wanted to play an icebreaker game as they had been mostly locked up since the pandemic, and then she unexpectedly dropped the fact that her boyfriend was heading over with her.

"Hey, I'm Destiny and this is my boyfriend, Sean."

"Hey, this is Jeremy and Devin. I'm Tim."

"Great to meet you all."

She gave them all googly eyes like you give someone at the end of the night when you wanted them to take you home, which was bizarre with her boyfriend there. He didn't seem to mind, such great hospitality here in the Great White North.

"Sean has the icebreaker game on his phone, and it

randomly picks people from the table to either participate in an act or answer a provocative question," Destiny explained. "If you don't perform the task or answer the question honestly, you have to drink."

"Seems easy enough to follow along," Tim said as they nodded their heads.

The questions started out fairly innocent and got weirder as the night went on. Even the dares got more and more risky as the game progressed. Was this the design of the game, or was Sean making up questions and dares as he went? Tim learned the answer to that question when Sean was dared to kiss Tim's bare butt cheek at the table in front of a packed bar. Although Tim questioned this whole charade, he wasn't a punk who turned down a dare either.

Tim, Jeremy, and Devin parted ways with the couple at the end of the night and discussed which one of them the couple tried to take home.

The next day arrived, and they were excited to see a whale for the first time in their lives. They reached the dock where the whale-watching boat would leave, only to discover it was completely foggy. They couldn't even see a quarter of an American football field ahead of them in the water. It was a doomed excursion from the start. After talking to the workers there, they learned all the spots for the only boat leaving the dock while they were still in town the next day were already filled. The group decided they had to risk it, to get the proverbial biscuit.

They suited up in the warm waterproof gear, talked

among themselves while the lengthy safety message was given in French, and patiently waited for the English version to commence. The captain finally made his way over to talk to them exclusively, the only three English speakers out of the two boats leaving the dock, and Tim was concerned when the safety briefing took less than half of the time as the French version. Was English much easier to speak or were they missing vital safety information? Time would tell.

Their captain was an absolute riot. He was pulling out all of the classic comedy routines to keep them entertained, as they would most likely not be able to see any marine life due to the fog. His antics included the old "faking walking down a flight of stairs behind a short wall" to get his coat. He had also pulled the classic "smashed up against the windshield" routine when he braked hard. Tim cried from laughter.

They sailed out onto the water and ten minutes into their journey the fog completely lifted in all directions. The clearing fog revealed the vast lake they were sailing on surrounded by picturesque mountains one would expect to see on a postcard. It felt like their boat captain was Moses and he had parted the seas.

There were kids on the other side of the boat who were screaming and pointing out into the water, "Fuck! Fuck!"

Tim shot a glance to the kid's parents and to the captain which hinted that they should reprimand these kids for their foul language. The parents joined in and encouraged the kids. This was completely shocking compared to how polite everyone was the entire time they had been there. Perhaps the secret to being polite as an adult was to encourage your kids to use foul language early on and get it out of their systems.

The captain noticed their concern and smacked his forehead as he walked over to them. "Please excuse their French. The kids are screaming phoque, it's the French word for seal."

The three native English speakers all laughed hysterically. That would be the joke for the rest of their trip. They saw a few whales that were attracted to the boat motors, which exceeded their expectations considering the gloomy outlook at the dock. Although the whales were smaller than Tim pictured before the trip, they were impressive as they were the largest sea animal he had seen in the wild before. They even stopped by the gift shop back at the dock and bought a few door mats that had a cute seal on them and read "PHOQUE OFF."

Their time in Canada had come to an end after another day of romping around Quebec City. The group was going to miss driving along the forests of pristine pine trees that seemed to go on forever in every direction. There wasn't this type of beauty in the city setting that they had come accustomed to and rarely ever ventured far from. They approached the United States border and had to wait in an interminable line this time around since they headed back home during normal hours. The interrogation process was stricter when they were trying to enter the United States, even though they were citizens of that great country.

The trip wouldn't end in Canada though, they planned

to visit Bar Harbor and Acadia National Park in Maine before they got back to their normal lives in Philadelphia. Jeremy was a big foodie and wanted to indulge in a lobster roll and also had a delicious pizza spot already selected in New Jersey on the way home.

The people in Bar Harbor were ruder than Tim imagined. He always heard the accents on TV and in film and thought it was just a stereotype; until he had been there and interacted with actual people who lived there. The owner of the restaurant where they got lobster rolls scolded them for an incomplete food order and blamed them for ordering separately. Not apologetic at all.

Acadia National Park was an absolute treasure, though. Tim thought he could live among the rude people in the area as long as it meant he could hike around the park anytime he wanted to. They had done a couple of easier and more lengthy hikes as soon as they got there. The group cooled off on the beach afterward with the famous Beehive trail hike towering over them as they dipped their toes in the water of the beach.

"Tomorrow, that mountain is ours," Devin said.

"I'll look at some videos of it tonight, but I don't think I'll be doing that hike," Jeremy replied.

"What? You're visiting Acadia and you're not going to do the coolest hike they have, which offers some of the best views of where we're standing right now?"

"I don't have a death wish, I'm not great with heights and people have definitely died in this park."

"Tim, I know you're not going to chicken out on me, are you?"

"My momma didn't raise any word that rhymes with witch."

Tim and his crew arrived at their campground where they were spending the night and grabbed some firewood from the front desk before they found their campsite. It was a large campground split into three sections. Their site was located next to a line of giant RVs and would make their twelve-person tent look miniscule in comparison. They had gotten the last campsite that was available which happened to be next to the bathrooms.

The three guys set up their tent with their three cots they had bought before the trip. Their industrial sized fan was plugged into their power strip all ready to drown out each other's snoring for the night. It was colder than they had imagined for that time of year and were hoping they wouldn't freeze to death in the middle of the night, if only they could start the fire inside the tent. Jeremy got the fire going outside and they sat around the campfire drinking some frosty beverages and passing around a bottle of Angel's Envy bourbon. Life was good.

The crew woke up the following morning; the earliest they had woken up on the entire trip to see the first sunrise experienced by anyone in the whole United States. They drove to the top of Cadillac Mountain in Acadia. Tim spouted off all his astronomy facts to anyone around him who was interested. He told them it takes eight minutes to travel from the sun to the Earth and that they were really seeing the sun as it was eight minutes ago. Tim spoke about how we could only see the next closest star to them as it was four-point-two years ago, but people started to not pay attention to him.

Tim couldn't believe that many people there had hiked up the mountain at the butt-crack of dawn that took forever for their car to ascend. The sunrise did not disappoint. They had driven down to the bottom of Beehive Mountain after the sunrise and Tim put the car in park.

"Are you sure you don't want to participate on what might be the coolest hike on the east coast?" Tim asked Jeremy.

"I watched a couple of videos last night. I absolutely don't want to. That hike your doing has some insane vertical drop offs and you have to hold on to hunks of rebar sticking out of the rocks in certain places."

"Alright, it's your loss."

Tim got out of the driver's seat and handed Jeremy the key fob. "She's fickle sometimes, but take care of her."

"I'm going to start packing up the tent and whatnot while you are hiking. Let me know when you're on the way back down and I'll head back to pick you up."

"Sounds good."

Devin and Tim climbed the mountain after their view of the sunrise. They were there before all of the people who hiked up Cadillac Mountain could catch up with them and certainly before the general public would get there. They had the trail all to themselves. The trail up was much more vertical than Tim had imagined, he did not watch any videos to prepare themselves before this day.

Tim grabbed the rebar sticking out of the rocks three quarters of the way up when he decided to finally look down instead of up and froze in absolute terror as he saw how high they were.

"Grab my hand, I'll help you up," said Devin.

Tim grabbed Devin's hand as his other hand slipped on the rebar. They tumbled down the side of the mountain until they landed on the car of a lovely couple from York, Pennsylvania. Jeremy never received a text from Tim to come pick them up and only discovered what had happened three hours later when he pulled up to the yellow police tape with the tent all packed up in the trunk of Tim's crossover vehicle.

Dominican Republic

(April 2016)

The cruise crew had been traveling with each other for a few years and finally planned their first trip that wasn't on a boat. A Punta Cana resort was similar to the boat life in its all-inclusive nature, minus all the cruise ports and the cruise director periodically bothering you throughout the day.

Thomas and Darian had taken Spanish in high school and brushed up before the trip since most of the workers at their resort would only know Spanish. Kyle cursed his parents for having him learn German, so he relied on Thomas and Darian for translations during this trip. Thomas and Darian taught him little phrases and words along the way, and Kyle made attempts. Not great attempts, but attempts, nonetheless.

As Thomas and Darian were teaching Kyle Spanish, they came up with a sinister plot to play a trick on him. Darian told Kyle that "como se dice" meant what is your name instead of "como se llama." They waited until the perfect moment presented itself.

Kyle wanted to call Darian an idiot in Spanish. Both Darian and Thomas could have given him other words which were close to the same meaning, however, they wanted to take Kyle's training wheels off and let him fend for himself.

"Go ahead, use your new skills to ask our server how to say idiot in Spanish," said Thomas.

"Here she comes, now is your chance," added Darian.

"Hola, inglés?" their server asked.

"Si, primero, como se llama, idiot?" Kyle asked politely.

The server gasped and stormed off.

"Who peed in her cereal this morning?" asked Kyle.

Thomas and Darian laughed and laughed for minutes at the exchange before Thomas could finally explain. "You asked that poor lady, what's your name, idiot?"

Darian almost fell off of his chair as another burst of laughter erupted from the two.

"That is so messed up," Kyle finally said when the laughter died down. "We're going to be here for an entire week and she'll probably be working and staring me down the entire time. Plotting my murder."

The resort featured three massive swimming pools where each had at least one swim-up bar, where they could order unlimited amounts of anything their hearts desired. This resort had more of an international appeal so there were people from all different countries there. There was a dance club on site and enough uniquely themed restaurants you could book reservations for each day, so you could have a different type of cuisine each day of the week. The beach that extended out from the resort was topless, however, there were "NO NUDITY" signs posted all around the pools in different languages.

The squad was by the main pool later that day, and Kyle kept noticing a lady who must have been in her forties glancing at him longer than normal. She didn't look like she was in her forties, but she had two kids with her who were apparently of drinking age. Kyle didn't notice a ring around her finger or another man with them. He swam in closer to investigate.

"Family vacation?" Kyle asked.

"Yes, those are my two children over there. I had them earlier on in life and haven't settled down with anyone else since."

Jackpot, Kyle thought.

"That's too bad. I don't understand how someone as gorgeous as you could be single, Ms. ..."

"I'm Rosa, and you?"

"Kyle, pleasure to meet you. Where are you from?"

"Originally, here. Santo Domingo to be more specific. Now we're in New Jersey. We come back here to visit family every once in a while. We tell them we're only in town for a few days and then spend a few days after we hang out with them at a resort like this in Punta Cana. How about you?"

"Wow, that's smart. I'm in Delaware. What a small world. We could create quite a life together after this."

Kyle pictured their house together in the suburbs with the white picket fence and a couple of dogs running around in the yard. Rosa was watering the garden and he was mowing the lawn as Rosa's kids, who were about the same age as Kyle, came home from college to stay with them for the weekend. They would come back here to the resort where they met every year to visit her family and lie to them about the length of their stay. A true fairytale.

"Please, I have kids who are almost your age."

Rosa swam away after her son yelled something in Spanish that Kyle didn't understand. All of Kyle's hopes and dreams he had pictured in his mind with his third girl of the day flushed down the toilet. How would he ever go on with life in this paradise? An inflatable beach volleyball struck his head to end that thought process as he moved on to the next potential prospect.

Kyle was unsuccessful the rest of the day. Later that afternoon, he took a shower to get ready for dinner. Though he heard the resort water was safe to drink, he paid special attention to keep his mouth closed. He noticed a small little abscess on his hip and popped it, he could never leave things like that alone, and scrubbed it sufficiently with soap.

They got dressed in their finest warm weather formal wear and went to a luau on the beach. This was after a few more drinks in them from the Italian restaurant they decided to kick the week off with. Kyle snuck off to reflect on losing Rosa earlier in the day and looked out to the beach to see her right in front of his eyes. She was sitting on a beach chair by herself. This was his chance.

"Hey, New Jersey, is this seat over here taken?"

"Just taken by you. I was hoping you would continue with your pursuit," Rosa said with a seductive tone.

"I thought I was too young?"

"I didn't want it to be too easy."

"Now that's out of the way. How about we head back to my room?"

"I would, but I'm sick right now."

"That's fine. I have this youthful immune system."

After hours of playful talk and whispering sweet nothings, Kyle would later find out she wasn't sick at all. Thomas was staying in Kyle's room with him and had to wait outside of their room for an entire hour as they handled their business. Her illness was not a traditional sickness; it was a monthly occurrence which required Kyle to call up room service for a change of sheets before Rosa would allow Thomas back in. Rosa left and Kyle wouldn't stop recapping his amazing night he had until he could hear Thomas snoring on his brand-new bed sheets.

Rosa disappeared after that day. The night before must have been her last day at the resort, and she figured she would go out with a bang. Kyle had the rug pulled out from under him again.

He thought about Rosa as he scrolled through his dating app on his phone the next night. His search radius was set on one mile, as he was trying to find someone else on the resort to meet up with. It didn't look like this dream scenario would pan out the way it did with Rosa. He heard going off the resort was a death sentence. However, so many stunning, local women were at the two-mile range. Some of them even had prices already listed on their profile and were strictly business. No falling in love and a clean breakaway was what he needed.

Kyle chatted a few of them up and could tell they were all using translator apps or were possibly the same person running different accounts. One girl in particular, though, caught his eye. She reminded him of a younger Rosa and was saying all the right things. The words were definitely going through a translation app; however, she didn't have prices listed and appeared to be genuine in her intent. He could make her fall in love and promise her a new life back in the United States, where she could become an elementary school teacher. They could have the white picket fence and the dogs and then maybe twenty years later, the kids could come back and visit from college. They would come back here to visit her family every year and lie about how long they were in town for so they could spend a few days alone at the resort where it all began.

He thought about what his parents would say if he brought someone home from vacation. More importantly, what would his girlfriend say? Yikes.

Kyle decided to make the arrangements. He knew the guys would never agree to let him go to see a lady of the night by himself off the resort. Kyle told them he was taking a taxi to go see a friend who was staying at another resort nearby, but he was actually walking to the front gate of the resort to meet up with Marta.

He convinced the guards he knew what he was doing after they tried to sway him out of his decision. Even they knew it was not a wise decision for tourists to leave the resort. Kyle had to meet up with Marta. He walked past the next level of guards with their rifles and began questioning his decision. Kyle was already committed. His heart felt like it would race right out of his chest and keep going if he stopped walking. There she was with her driver, as promised, in the little green sedan she said she would be in.

"Hola!" Marta greeted him.

"Hello, I guess you don't speak English?"

"No hablo inglés."

"Uno momento." Kyle was getting the hang of the Spanish language now. He pulled out his phone and typed the first message to her in his translator app.

"Where are we going?"

"I was thinking a hotel close by."

"Why not my resort?"

"They won't let me enter the resort unless you pay for me for as long as you're staying."

"The hotel sounds good."

Kyle had the time of his life in the crusty looking—most likely funded by the hour—hotel room with the younger Rosa. That's right, Marta.

Afterwards, she looked at him lovingly in the eyes and whispered, "Dinero?"

Kyle knew what that meant in English. He had completely forgotten about that part of the equation and knew he didn't have any local currency since they hadn't planned on leaving the resort. He glanced down at his wallet, which he pointed away from Marta, and didn't like what he saw. There was only a crisp Benjamin in there. It was his only option and he handed it over to her hoping his experience wasn't that expensive. He also was hoping it would be enough, he didn't want to know what would follow if it wasn't enough.

"Is that enough?"

"Uno memento, por favor."

Marta put on some clothes and left the room. He could hear her sprint down the stairs and entered into a heated discussion with a masculine sounding voice. Trepidation fell over Kyle as he felt like he had insulted her as if it wasn't enough for the experience with her and the hotel room. What would he do if Marta and the other voice came storming into the room asking for more money. Was there an ATM nearby that could save him? Or perhaps it was too much, and they were scheming ways to kidnap him and hold him as a bribe to make some real money off of him. Maybe he should put on his clothes and look around for anything that could be considered a weapon to defend himself.

The minutes felt like hours as he awaited his fate. The discussions finally concluded, and Kyle suddenly heard footsteps coming up the stairs. It sounded like one set of footsteps. That was good. Marta entered the room with a businesslike demeanor which morphed into a smile.

"Está bien," she said.

Kyle was finally at ease and their driver took them back to his resort to drop him off. He and Marta continued to use his phone translator app the entire trip to continue their awkward conversation. Kyle felt like the luckiest boy in the world now that his little escapade had worked out safely, besides the fact that his midsection was starting to feel sore. He figured it was most likely from all the action he had been getting during this week of hedonism. He got back to the resort, showered, and slept like a baby that night.

Kyle woke up to another message from Marta.

"Can we meet again?"

"Absolutely."

"One hour? Out front?"

"Perfecto."

Kyle was in love with this girl. He wanted the guys to meet Marta. Kyle spent the entire morning at breakfast bragging to the guys about what he actually did the previous night, which was met with plenty of positive reinforcement.

He strolled up to the front gates of the resort after breakfast to meet her again as they planned. Kyle had the intention of surprising her by paying for her to stay at the resort with him for the rest of his vacation. He would have to make sure the other guys didn't get any ideas about his woman while she stayed with them.

He hopped in the same car which was there for him the previous day to tell her his plan. Before he could speak, they sped off. Their driver from the previous day did not look happy and Marta didn't have the most inviting expression on her face either.

"That wasn't enough money last night," the driver said in perfect English.

Apparently, the driver, who was silent all of yesterday, did speak English.

"Where are we going?" asked Kyle, scared out of his mind.

"I'm taking you to an ATM right now."

"I don't have my wallet. I left it back in the room." Kyle lied, saying whatever to get himself out of this situation.

"Alright, I'm taking you back to the resort and waiting outside of your room until you grab it. You need to convince the guards to let me in."

"What am I going to tell them?"

"I don't know, but you better figure it out."

The driver dropped Marta off at a local restaurant; she had fulfilled her duties of making Kyle trust them again. Kyle got his driver in the resort after telling the guards he had to grab something quickly before they headed into town. They got to his building on the resort and Kyle dashed into his room and locked the door behind him.

He paced around the room knowing his life was on the line. He peered out of his blinds every ten seconds, hoping for some reason that the driver's car wouldn't be there every time he looked out. Eventually, by some kind of divine intervention, a worker at the resort had security come over and remove the driver from the area. Kyle jumped up and down and danced around the room until a new message from Marta popped up on his phone.

"We will find you. You can't stay at that resort forever."

Kyle spent the rest of his stay at the resort with this soul-crushing feeling weighing him down. He knew the driver would be waiting for him outside of the resort when he and the guys left for the airport. Should he make up some weird excuse to head to the airport early to not involve the other guys in his predicament? He could be honest with the others, and they might rally around him to defend him on the way to the airport. Maybe he could stay at the resort forever? The driver told him he couldn't do that, and it made Kyle want to defy him.

He couldn't tell if the throbbing pain in his abdomen was from the nervousness in leaving the resort, or the muscles he had utilized twice on vacation. Kyle had been feeling febrile the last day and was assuming it was from being out in the sun for too long. He was never going to cheat on his girlfriend ever again if he actually made it home safely.

"Hey man, you don't look so good. Are you alright?" Thomas asked.

"I'm fine," Kyle replied. "I just really don't want to go home."

The three jumped into their taxi when it arrived, a large twelve-passenger van which had more than enough room for them with all of their luggage in the back. Kyle climbed into the third row of seats immediately after storing his luggage and Thomas and Darian were in the second row of seats. The van pulled away from their building and crept toward the gate and the guards who Kyle had come to know over a few occasions. He was frantically scanning the surrounding areas beyond the guard shack and spotted the car and man who had been driving him around earlier in the week. The driver was leaning up against his car with his arms folded looking like a lion that was stalking one particular impala. Kyle expeditiously ducked down and laid on the bench seating in the third row.

"This had been a long week, I think I'm going to take a nap," Kyle nervously announced over to the second row of seating where Thomas and Darian were seated.

"It's not that far to the airport," Darian replied.

"Just a little cat nap, wake me up when we're there."

Sweat poured out of Kyle, he was stricken with fear every time the van paused. Kyle assumed every local, including his current driver, was colluding against him in an effort to extort him for the money he owed. He wasn't actually tired when he laid down, but the emotional strain along with his fever eventually caused him to pass out in the third row. Thomas and Darian weren't able to wake him up once they reached the airport. The staph infection from his abscess he picked at in the shower earlier in the week had reached his blood stream, and it was too late to save him by the time they reached the closest hospital. Kyle didn't cheat on his girlfriend ever again after that day.

Spain

(September 2022)

The last stop of a five-country outing was here, and what better way to end a trip than in beautiful Barcelona. Amanda and Lexi chose a place between their visit in Austria and their cheap flight home before a layover in Portugal. Lexi expected Spanish to be the primary language when she arrived at the airport, only to find out Catalan was the first choice. They later found out they would be in town for one of the biggest festivals of the year: La Mercè Festival.

Their place was located on the sixth floor of a vintage-style modernist building that looked like it dated back to the early twentieth century. It featured a sunny and spacious terrace which invited anyone to enjoy it at any time of the day, and was the selling point that drew them in. It was an unbeatable location which could comfortably fit up to four people. There was a beautiful mixture of modern and contemporary furniture throughout and two bedrooms with double beds.

Their first stop was to see the famous Sagrada Família,

a Roman Catholic church designed by the famous Catalan architect Antoni Gaudí. Construction began on the church in 1882 and continues until this day in 2023. Gaudí knew he would not be alive to oversee the full construction of the church and left detailed designs to guide its completion. Amanda and Lexi were across the street from the impressive church taking pictures from every angle.

"Do you want to see if we can get tickets to go inside?" asked Amanda.

"Eh, not really." Lexi shrugged. "Once you've seen one church inside, you've seen them all."

"We came all this way and we're going to stop across the street from it?"

"More long benches and stained glass, what could be much different about this one? Plus, it's an active construction site and I heard there's a super sketchy spiral staircase on the inside. I'm not trying to die on this trip."

"We're already here. Why not pay a few bucks and check it out? We can leave immediately if you're unimpressed."

Amanda still owed Lexi some money as Lexi fronted most of the trip so they could be on the same boarding passes and for general ease of planning. Lexi was bothered that Amanda wanted to spend money when she had an outstanding balance between them. She tried not to show it since there was more time left in the trip. She also didn't want Amanda to forget about paying her back after the trip though, as she assumed Amanda would.

"Just more time and money," Lexi said. "I know I'm not going to be impressed. I came to see the outside. That did not disappoint."

"Would you wait for me if I went inside?" Amanda asked.

"I'm not going to lie. Probably not. I would probably start walking to Parc Güell and you can catch a taxi and meet me there. I know you hate walking so it's a win for both of us. Plus, I have to get my boss some ibuprofen cream before I leave Barcelona, and I can try to knock that out on the way. It's going to be fun trying to order this stuff in Spanish at the pharmacy and I don't want you to see it."

"I do not want to get separated, let's walk there together now."

"Are you sure? I don't want you complaining the whole way because you didn't go inside the church and that your feet hurt and you're tired."

"Let's just go, but I can't promise I won't complain."

The ladies set off on their walk to Parc Güell, which Amanda assured Lexi was around the corner. Amanda's around the corner and Lexi's around the corner were two completely different definitions. Amanda didn't account for the fact that it was mostly uphill also.

The street intersections in many areas didn't allow a pedestrian to walk in a straight path toward their destination. The buildings and sidewalks at every crossing cut in at a forty-five-degree angle before the crosswalk, causing a person to walk in a zig-zag pattern. Each intersection looked octagonal from a satellite image, like a stop sign if paying attention to the sidewalks and crosswalks exclusively. This was aggravating for Amanda and Lexi and they were met with many peculiar looks when they walked in a straight path through the busy streets without bending in to utilize the crosswalks.

"My map is saying we're right next to it. One more block, I swear," Lexi reassured Amanda.

"You've been saying that for the last three blocks. My legs are tired. I didn't get to see the church. I'm hungry. I'm sober. I didn't wear the right shoes for this," Amanda said each phrase in between gasping for air.

"There it is!" Lexi interrupted her. "It was just the back entrance to the park. I wasn't expecting that. Apparently, you have to pay too, which sucks."

"Well let's get in line before they close."

Amanda and Lexi walked over toward the long queue to stand in line for the ticket booth and were greeted with workers bringing out the "SORRY, WE'RE CLOSED" signs.

"You have got to be kidding me, you made me walk all this way and it's closing?" Amanda rhetorically asked.

"Well, it would have been even worse if you went into the church," Lexi retorted.

"I have an idea. They can't deny us entry if we already have tickets for the day. Let's go online and see if we can snag tickets and tell them we had purchased them earlier today."

"That's crazy enough to work. I have had terrible reception all trip though."

"I already had the website pulled up on my phone. Two tickets, credit card info, and got it!"

"Alright, let's see if this works."

The two walked up to the gate and waltzed right past the employees at the gate and all of the other disappointed guests who were standing in the ticket line complaining to the workers. They could see a few people following their lead and pulling out their phones to use the same trick. Amanda and Lexi didn't have a ton of time once they were in the park, regardless, it was totally worth the adventure and all downhill from where they entered through the back entrance. They called it an early night after all of the exercise and mental stress they experienced on their first day.

The next morning, they researched the events at the festival to see what they could check out and saw there was a people stacking event. Amanda and Lexi had no idea what it meant, however, they had to see this. There were many different stages spread throughout the city that had a plethora of different musical performances. They would try to see as much as they could before their free walking tour commenced and then pick up where they left off afterward. The two ladies walked down Las Ramblas past Mercat de la Boqueria to see if they could check out the festivities. They couldn't believe all of the dogs were running around without leashes, and how well they behaved while not straying too far from their owners.

They stopped on the way to the festival to make a rum and coke mixture to deal with the crowds. Lexi couldn't believe all of the items in the store they stopped at had so few ingredients, compared to the millions of ingredients you can't even read that make up American food. The only downside was having to pay for grocery bags.

The areas where the parade ran were packed wall to wall, and it got pushy as they were being squished in between people. The rum and coke mixture kicked in as it got hard to breathe in the stale air between buildings. They both knew to have all of their belongings in their front pockets and to wear their backpacks in their front side to prevent any theft. The crowd finally dispersed when the funny giant costumes of people finally ended.

"I think it's happening," Amanda said as she pointed in the direction of the town square.

There was a ring of sturdy looking men who were climbing on top of the shoulders of an even sturdier looking group of men. There was even a layer of the sturdiest men under that level. Next, robust looking women began climbing up the backs of the circles of men to form a smaller circle on their shoulders and this continued for another two levels. The tower of people was massive and led all the way up to a single lady on top.

"No way," Amanda muttered.

Lexi gasped. "That's a child climbing to the top!"

"At least she's wearing a helmet."

They could see the sturdy men at the bottom layers of the tower tremble and it spread up the tower like it was contagious. The child had her arms around the lone female at the top and shimmied her body until she stood directly on top of her shoulders and held up four fingers straight in the air. The crowd went wild. The tower of people did everything in the exact opposite order and were met with thunderous applause when they were safely at the bottom.

"Woah, that was incredible," Lexi said.

"I can't believe they sent a child up to the top."

"If there's a way, we can sign up to try that, we're doing it."

"Absolutely not."

The ladies were so excited they got to see such an amazing feat and wanted to stay around for more of the parade, but they had a free walking tour of the city to catch. They fought their way through the crowds and met their tour guide on the outskirts of the gothic quarter right before the tour was about to commence. The gothic quarter was a charming labyrinthian of streets, medieval architecture, and historic public squares.

"Gustave Eiffel originally pitched his tower to the city of Barcelona, Spain. They rejected it. They were worried it would be an unwieldy eyesore and the cost was too high," the tour guide said as they were walking along the gothic quarter. "They have this funny tradition here where people buy little figurines called a Caganer of different famous people defecating, and put it inconspicuously among a nativity scene during Christmas time."

Their tour guide was extremely charismatic and explained the damages earthquakes had incurred on the old buildings over the years. "If you look up you can see the damaged heavy statues all along the roofline of this church. They have detached randomly over the years and have killed and maimed a few people that were unfortunate enough to be standing under them when it happens."

The tour guide pointed at a woman who was standing directly under a statue. "Kind of like how she is standing now …"

Silence fell over their tour group, and everyone stood with their mouths agape waiting for the woman's impending doom.

After an awkward ten seconds, Lexi finally interrupted, "That's so messed up."

"I guess today's not the day." The tour guide continued walking.

Amanda and Lexi were near the back of their tour group strolling along Santa María del Mar. A church which was shaken by a major earthquake in 1428 that destroyed the large rose window killing twenty people. A large statue at the top of the church decided to dislodge itself and crushed the two ladies under its massive weight. There was a long history of statues falling off of buildings due to damages caused by earthquakes and it had been decades since there was an incident. Today was not their lucky day.

Australia

(December 2018)

Bridget was stoked to take the next thirteen-hour leg of her trip from San Francisco to Auckland, New Zealand on her way to Sydney, Australia. As if the previous four-hour leg of her journey wasn't enough, she spent more than half a day cramped in her window seat next to a smelly person, too afraid to leave her seat, even for bathroom breaks, to not disturb the man with the questionable odor. She had the perfect mix of airport beverages to dehydrate herself to accomplish that goal. After her long odyssey through four airports, she finally landed on the opposite side of the planet.

Her adventure started in the frigid winter temperatures of Omaha, Nebraska and ended in the one-hundred-degree-Fahrenheit freak heat wave in Australia. Her jeans and sweater she wore to brave her trip to the first airport, and survive the cold airplanes, were now trying to cause her to have a heat stroke.

She got to her hotel and laid in her comfy bed and fought as hard as she could not to go to sleep immediately at six p.m. She didn't sleep much on the planes but wanted to survive a bit longer to acclimate herself to the new time zone. After narrowly avoiding defeat, she decided to head to the hotel bar to distract herself for an extra couple of hours before an early bedtime and a lengthy hibernation. First, she went into her bathroom and flushed the toilet to see if the water did spin in the opposite direction in the southern hemisphere. To her disappointment, the water rushed in from the back, flushed down, and didn't spin in either direction.

"How you going?" asked the bartender.

"I'll take an old fashioned."

"Let me get you a menu first." The bartender held a finger in the air.

As he handed her the menu, she noticed his nametag read "Chaz." Instead of looking at the menu, she stared at Chaz as he polished glassware. Chaz pretended not to recognize her stare and returned after polishing a stemmed wine glass.

"What are you thinking about ordering?" Chaz asked.

"I think I'll take an old fashioned, *Chaz*."

"No worries. Coming right up."

"Thanks, *Chaz*."

"You seem a little uptight. Are you from the United States?"

Bridget was mildly offended by the question, *are we that easy to spot and unpleasant to be around?* "How did you know?"

"We're more laid back here in Australia. You'll learn our ways if you spend enough time here."

"We'll see about that."

"What brings you here? Holiday?"

"You mean vacation? Yes."

"Who are you traveling with?"

Chaz finished the old fashioned and placed it in front of Bridget.

"Just me. I recently got out of a breakup and decided to come out here and find myself."

"Wow. Long way from home. You can be whoever you want to be all the way out here."

"I would like to be myself right now. As in by myself, without you asking me questions."

"No worries." Chaz walked away to check on a couple of other customers at the bar.

Bridget was finally back in her room after a couple of drinks, avoiding small talk with the bartender. For how invasive and pretentious Chaz was, he did make an incredible old fashioned. He said she could be anyone she wanted to be since she was this far away from home. She browsed through her unlimited swipe rights on her dating app, waiting for exhaustion to overtake her when the old fashioned took effect. She thought about the bartender's words and decided, why not. She changed the "Looking For" option on her app to "Male or Female."

Bridget left her home on a Friday and didn't arrive until Sunday; she missed an entire day flying, and it was starting to impart its effects on her. She thought about how it would be weird traveling the opposite way to get home. She would travel for the same amount of time, twenty-four whole hours, and it would still be the same day after crossing the international date line. As interesting as this thought was, sleep deprivation soon won.

Bridget woke up the next morning with a flood of notifications from her dating app. There didn't seem to be a clear winner, but the males outweighed the number of female matches. She must have seemed exotic to all of the people here with her sexy American accent and physical features. Those folks from the United States do have the best accents.

One message from her dating app stood out, Ava from Australia. She sent Ava a message along with a few other runners-up and took a shower to start with her packed itinerary she planned for the day. Her limited time in Sydney was packed with a surf lesson in the shark infested waters and tours to see the amazing Bondi Beach, the Sydney Opera House, and the Sydney Harbor Bridge. First, a beverage to calm her nerves before the surf lesson. She went to the hotel bar to hopefully see her good buddy Chaz again.

"Let me get some Australian wine this morning, no questions this time."

"No menu? Bold strategy. Coming right up," Chaz replied.

"Thanks."

"She's not here to fuck spiders," Chaz quietly said as he grabbed the wine.

"Are there really a lot of sharks in the waters around here?" Bridget asked.

"Oh yeah, they're everywhere. They put shark nets in

place for all of you outsiders during the tourist season though."

Bridget was ready to cancel her plans for the day after hearing that. "For real?"

"No, they don't put nets out, that would be too much work and it would harm wildlife."

"Are you serious?"

"Yes, make sure you have your thongs and sunnies with you if you're heading to the beach in the arvo."

"Excuse me?" Bridget asked with an offended tone.

"Ah, we say thongs instead of flip-flops here. Sunnies, sunglasses. Arvo, short for afternoon."

"Seems like a pretty lazy way to talk here."

"It's not the sharks you should worry about, though."

"What should I worry about?"

"You should worry more when you're on land."

"What's on land?"

"Drop bears."

"Drop bears?"

"Absolutely, koala bears hang up in trees, all cute and cuddly, only to drop down on unsuspecting people and take them out."

"For real?"

"Nope, I'm just messing with you, mate."

"Stop talking to me."

"For real for real, and not foreplay. You're going to want to check your shoes every time you put them on."

"Why would I do that?"

"It's not a big problem in the cities, but you're going to want to make sure there aren't any of our many deadly snakes or spiders that have found their way in there and made a home out of your shoes. Check both the right and left shoe."

"Lovely. I was assuming they didn't have a right or left preference."

"No worries, mate."

Little did Chaz know, Bridget was, in fact, full of worries.

Bridget was never a big wine person, however, the Australian wine she had for breakfast was incredible. Maybe it was the fear speaking and it tasted like the last beverage she would have on Earth. Regardless, she was going to have to consider bringing some back home with her to share with her mother. That would cause her to check a bag though, Bridget was antipathetic to checking bags whenever she traveled. Unless she absolutely had to.

Bridget showed up to her surf lesson way too early. She was still nervous about the sharks even after her morning beverage and her unwanted troubling conversation with the bartender. Bridget walked into a cute little shop by Bondi Beach and stared dumbfoundedly at the menu above the counter.

"What's vegemite?" Bridget asked the gentleman behind the counter.

"If you have to ask, you don't want to get it. Trust me," he replied.

"Do you really eat ground kangaroo meat here too? And throw it on the barbie? Or the barbeque?"

"It's lean so it's mostly a bodybuilder thing, we have

it here though."

"I've been working out a little, but I'm certainly not a bodybuilder. One scone and an Americano, please."

"One Americano, for the cute little Americano."

Bridget handed her credit card to the employee behind the counter, and he waved it over the credit card machine.

"What are you doing?" Bridget asked.

"Is this not a tap and go?"

"A what? You just swipe it."

"Ah, we have had contactless payment via credit card for some time now. You Americans will catch up eventually."

These Australians were so cheeky. Everyone talked to her like they had known Bridget for decades and had inside jokes with her before even meeting. She downed her coffee and threw away the scone after only taking one bite as she was still too anxious about her lesson. The coffee only made her anxiety worse, faster now. What was she thinking?

Arriving at the surf shop, Bridget was fitted with a wet suit and given a surfboard, which was a different color and larger than the other people in the group. She wasn't sure what to make of that. If she was swept out to sea, she would be able to invite Jack onto this giant surfboard to save him from Davy Jones's locker. Her classmates were all of European origin and were skinnier than her, regardless, Bridget felt strong as she had been training her core for some time before this day.

They were given the safety briefings and headed out into the water. Bridget felt better as there were many local surfers who were much farther out in the swell than she would be. The sweeping white sand beach was a crescent moon shape and wasn't far from each side where the land curved back inwards, easily walkable. Bridget had been used to the beaches back home that went on for miles in a straight line where you couldn't even see both ends. She was riding the waves and standing up on her board successfully for a solid half an hour before they were brought back in for a short break from the water.

The instructor grabbed her surfboard from her. "This thing is way too easy for you, it's like riding in a wave on a picnic table."

"Then why did you give it to me?" asked Bridget.

"You're a big dumb American, I was only expecting you to fake drown and try to sue me."

"That's fair. It's the third time I've heard something similar on this trip already."

"Here you go. This is the board everyone else is using."

They headed back out after fifteen minutes with the new surfboard, and it was harder for her to ride on it. The instructor was right, the bigger board was more like a picnic table than a surfboard. Bridget didn't see one shark the entire time she was out in the water, even though she felt a few questionable things rub against her. Afterward, she bought a sick picture from their photographer to change her dating app profile so she would fit in with the locals.

When she finally checked her phone, Ava had sent her a couple of messages. Bridget wanted to see if she could keep up and invited her to go climb the Sydney Harbor

Bridge with her for a first date. She copied and pasted the message into a few other chats that were open and went for a stroll onto Bondi Beach.

She didn't meet with any of her matches on the bold first dates she offered them. She did hang out with a stag party for most of the night who repeatedly used the C word, which was apparently common for everyone to use. Sydney had been good to Bridget; however, all good things must eventually come to an end. It was time for her to head to the next city on her extended holiday.

The first stop on her trip near Brisbane was Fraser Island, the largest sand island and home of eighteen different snake species, though only a third of them are venomous and dangerous to humans. Not to mention the crocs, dingoes, and various other lizards who inhabited the island. The island is surrounded by great white sharks and the vicious Portuguese Man o' War. Definitely no worries here. Bridget only saw a few dingoes from a distance and got to float down a natural lazy river on one part of the huge island.

After all the wild and dangerous animals she saw the previous day, it was time for a completely different experience at a koala sanctuary. She got to hold a koala and took the perfect picture with it to make her friends back home jealous. Her social media post read "Having a beary good time," though they weren't bears but marsupials. Koalas hold on tighter to people with more muscles as they grip onto them like they would the bark of a tree. Bridget got a confidence boost since it held on tightly to her. She approached the koala sanctuary sign with a behemoth spider above, but was informed it was not part of the exhibit.

The third stop on the itinerary was the incredible rainbow beach. Bridget relaxed by the magnificently colored sand dunes and waited until the amazing sun set closed out the night. She remained there after the sun stopped illuminating the area and the Milky Way made its incredible presence across the night sky.

Bridget had never seen the band of the Milky Way galaxy before and thought about how incredibly small and rare intelligent life was among the vast cosmos. It brought tears to her eyes to think how lucky she was to be born and given the opportunity to explore this Earth. She was living her life to the fullest and nothing could hold her back after this awe-inspiring experience. She could lay there all night but worried about all the dangerous animal species that might come out.

Her time in Sydney and Brisbane was the experience of a lifetime and although she'd love to visit again someday, she had spent her time wisely and didn't feel the need to come back. Bridget's airport ride pulled up to her apartment, and the gentleman jumped out of the car to help her with her luggage.

"Heading to the airport?" her driver asked.

"Sadly," Bridget replied.

"What time is your flight?"

"In two hours."

"Wow, you're heading to the airport way too early."

"It's international, so I'm a little behind on how early I usually get to the airport."

"You're going to have no trouble at all."

Her driver tossed her luggage in the trunk as she walked to the front of the car to get in the passenger's side. This guy was friendly enough. Why not sit up front? She opened the door and noticed the steering wheel on her side.

"Are you going to drive us there?"

Bridget was offended at first, but she was used to being embarrassed by each one of her blunders. "Oh yeah. You drive on the wrong side here. I completely forgot."

"No worries."

Bridget couldn't believe she was already back at the airport after her first solo travel experience in a whole different hemisphere. Her airline wouldn't let her check in with her phone and needed to check in at the counter; what a bummer. She walked over to the counter with her small personal item backpack and her two-wheeled carry-on.

"How you going?" the airline employee asked.

"Sad that I have to leave this beautiful country," Bridget replied.

"Can you throw your bag on the scale for me?"

Bridget confidently tossed her two-wheeled bag onto the scale. She made a spreadsheet for the different carry-on requirements of each airline she took before the trip and made sure her bags were precisely under the required dimensions and weight limits. She switched some items around, so they were no longer in the same position when she originally left the United States.

"This bag is one kilogram over the limit."

"It's so close, it's going on the plane either way."

"I'm sorry, you can try to rearrange some of your luggage from this bag to your backpack and try again."

Bridget let out an exaggerated sigh. "And stand in line again? Can't you let it slide?"

"I don't make the rules. I just enforce them."

Bridget stormed away from the counter to shift things between her bags. She always kept a change of clothes in her backpack in case the checked bag didn't make it, but she hoped to avoid checking a bag at all. After shuffling some things around with her bags sprawled out in the middle of the airport, she was back in line. She ended up at the counter of the same woman she was dealing with before.

"How you going?"

"Don't give me that. Just weigh my bag again."

"Point-five kilograms over. Would you like to check this bag?"

"This is ridiculous. I'm not going through this again. Go ahead and check it. My bag better be there when I get to New Zealand. I'm far away from the United States and all alone."

The airline employee attached the luggage tag to her bag and sent it on its way down the conveyor belt.

"Thanks for choosing our airline. We hope you have a safe trip."

"Yeah, yeah. No worries."

Bridget walked dejectedly over to the security line and

was through in less than three minutes. She didn't even have to take her shoes off and they let her through with the half full liter of water she had in the side pouch of her backpack. They definitely didn't have worries here.

There was plenty of time for Bridget to sample more of the delicious Australian wine on the other side of security. She decided to get a little alcohol buzz before the flight as she always did, but after she strolled by her assigned gate sober to make sure she could find it. Bridget found the perfect cozy bar near her gate. She thought about how lonely she was while her best friend Sarah and her boyfriend Chris explored the Nordic countries in Europe. She scrolled through her social media feed, waiting to see their engagement photos from the igloo with the glass roof under the northern lights in Norway that Sarah wouldn't stop talking about before the trip. They were probably on their cheap flight home from Sweden around this time, a much cheaper trip than Bridget's current itinerary.

New Zealand

(January 2019)

Bridget traveled from the land where basically every animal could kill you to the land where there weren't many animals that could kill you. The land where there were at least five sheep for every person living there and the home of the adorable kiwi. There weren't a lot of natural threats besides the terrain itself, so people had to invent ways to seek thrills. A place where adventure seekers flocked from all around the world.

She arrived back in Auckland, New Zealand at midnight and joined a bunch of apoplectic fellow passengers at the luggage carousel. The airline lost almost everyone's luggage. If only she would have tried to rearrange her bags again to not check her bag in Australia. She was furious at the airline employee who made her switch her clothes around which resulted in her barely having any clothes in her backpack. It was after midnight when she finally fought her way through the line at the lost luggage counter to fill in the appropriate forms. She would be moving around a bunch in New Zealand so they needed to send her luggage to a different location depending on the day they found it.

Bridget grabbed her keys at the rental company desk after an ephemeral wait and inspected her vehicle. The only thing Bridget could see wrong with the car was the steering wheel on the wrong side. She contemplated getting a manual transmission for the full experience, she was grateful she decided against that, given her current sleep deprived and perturbed mental state.

She reminded herself at every intersection: Right hand turns are difficult now. Left hand turns are easy now. She slowly navigated the mostly abandoned streets at that time of night, staying on the correct side of the road the entire way. She made it all the way to her apartment, staying under all the posted kilometer per hour signs she was not used to. Bridget messaged her host, hoping she'd let her use her washer and dryer.

"Just got in the apartment, amazing setup! So my checked bag with most of my clothes got lost at the airport. I know I'm not staying for seven days required to use the washer and dryer, but would you mind if I threw a bookbag worth of clothes in the washer/dryer? I can throw you some extra money or buy you some beer or something? I'm going to try to wake up at eight or so to either do that or go shopping for clothes. Also sorry for the late message, long day of traveling."

Bridget most likely wouldn't get a message back until the morning. Her place was a luxurious studio apartment in the heart of Manukau City. The place had bifolding French doors which opened completely onto the balcony that provided amazing views of the distant Manukau Harbour and Waitakere Ranges. The place was fully furnished with a large lounge, designer kitchen, island, and an immaculate bathroom. Bridget was sad she was only staying one night in this beautiful place.

She woke to a message from her host.

"Hi Bridget. Not a problem. You can definitely use the washer and dryer and there is no need for any payment. Go to the back of the house, left when you get out the door and walk all the way around. I have opened the ranch slider to the laundry. The washing powder is in the red container on the floor."

She cleaned the extra garments she brought in her backpack, along with the clothes she had on, after sneaking around back in her bra and panties to access the washer and dryer. A few hours later, with the two sets of clean clothes in her possession, it was time to head to the store where she grabbed another set of clothes and a towel for her zorbing experience. She hoped she'd only have to purchase the one set of souvenirs.

Her first stop in the adventure capital of the world was Rotorua on the North Island. An adventure park there featured many adrenaline pumping activities as well as the highest zorbing hill in the entire world. Though her first adventure was driving on the wrong side of the road in the daytime when there were more drivers. She managed to do fine after realizing there wasn't an abundance of drivers and most of the roads were single lane each way between more populated areas. There were long stretches with periodic passing zones. She noticed many people didn't wait until the passing zones and only passed slower drivers whenever the opportunity safely presented itself.

Her place in Rotorua was a bright and spacious open plan apartment featuring three beautifully appointed bedrooms. There was a private sun-soaked deck, modern bathroom featuring both bath and standalone shower, and a fully equipped kitchen. It was situated in the center of town, within walking distance to all the bars, restaurants, shops, local markets, cinemas, and the beloved Rotorua Lake. The lack of cleaning fee was nice too.

The only problem was getting inside of the place. The check-in instructions noted that the key was on a hook inside the shed on the backyard of the property.

Bridget thought how strange it must look for an outside observer to see her rummaging around the shed of a place she had never been before. It probably looked like she was a burglar trying to break in. Bridget was halfway toward working through the brush that led to the shed when she panicked thinking about a venomous snake hiding in the tall grass. She ran in terror until she remembered there weren't any dangerous animals in the land of kiwis. There might still be dangerous spiders there though, so she proceeded with caution. After a few attempts, she secured the key and got into her apartment.

Her first excursion in Rotorua would be the adventure park. She wanted to ride the downhill luge and ride one of the fastest zip lines straight down the mountainside. She couldn't believe helmets were only "recommended" at the downhill luge, especially coming from a culture in the United States where everyone sues for everything they can think of. The luge was super-fast. The downhill zip line, reaching speeds exceeding sixty kilometers per hour, did require a helmet and an insubstantial waiver. The only instructions were, "when the fog clears and you can see my friend at the end make sure you straighten your arms on the handles so you don't smash your teeth in." What a rush.

Bridget left the adventure park with her heart pounding. She wanted to stay there longer, but she wanted to Zorb downhill with the remaining time she had on her only day in town. She was at the front desk signing all the waiver forms when they asked her which experience she wanted.

"I want the big hill."

"That's the best one if you're only here for a short time. It's high as."

"High as what?" Bridget asked.

"Yeah, no. It's a thing we say here."

The worker guided her over to a beat-up pickup truck that would take them up to the top and they both jumped inside.

"I hope you're alright with freezing cold water. We haven't worked out a way to get hot water up this high in the hill yet," the employee said.

"Now you tell me, after I paid."

They reached the spot where the Zorb's were taking off from. There was another truck already there with a trailer filled with the giant plastic bubbles. There was another guy filling the Zorb inner chamber up with hose water. This process gave her plenty of time to look down the hill and remember she wasn't a big fan of heights.

"Are you sure you want to do this?"

"I came here to Zorb down the highest hill I could find, and fuck spiders. I don't see any spiders."

"A simple yes would have done."

Bridget dove into the side Zorb tube that led to the inner chamber and experienced a pain on her abdomen when she got inside. She got scratched on the zipper that closed the chamber and sealed her inside. Bridget began to wonder who else had been in this Zorb before her and if there was any way she could get infected with anything. It's too late now. They had already sealed the chamber and tipped her over the edge.

She rolled around in the Zorb for what felt like an eternity as she continuously picked up speed and couldn't figure out which way was up. The camera they had attached to her would certainly not show flattering footage. Bridget's stomach felt like it was about to come up out of her throat, but couldn't see any hues of red as she tumbled around and that was reassuring, at least her stomach scratch was fine. As quickly as she was thrust into this terrifying descent, it was over as she settled down on solid ground. She pondered the scratch on her abdomen as she waited for someone to come and let her out.

"I bet you can't wait to check out the footage!" a woman said as she unzipped the Zorb and let her out.

"I one hundred percent don't want to check that out."

She inspected herself and escaped with only minor injuries, for now.

When she received her belongings from the staff, she

had a voicemail from her airline. The nice lady on the other end stated that her bags were being flown via helicopter out to her in Rotorua. Perfect, right before she was heading back to Auckland airport where they were coming from. The bag was waiting for her outside of her place when she got back from her zorbing experience.

Bridget wanted to visit another famous hill in the North Island with the longest name she had ever seen called Taumatawhakatangihangakoauauotamateapokaiwhenuakitanatahu. The name translates to: the place where Tamatea, the man with the big knees, who slid, climbed and swallowed mountains, known as "landeater," played his flute to his loved one. Locals around there simply call it Taumata Hill. Bridget amusingly wanted to go take a picture with the sign, she didn't have enough time though.

Bridget did have enough time to cruise down the rivers inside of the Waitomo Caves before she left the North Island. An extensive network of caves you can walk or drift through and view the thousands of glow-worms which illuminate the completely dark underground ceilings. Bridget looked up and was reminded of her incredible experience of seeing the Milky Way galaxy on Rainbow Beach in Australia, and again felt ecstatic to be alive on this wonderful planet.

A few days had passed since Bridget arrived in New Zealand and she was now in the South Island after another flight with all of her possessions she had initially traveled with. Bridget did not have to check her bag this time. She also had her fresh New Zealand wardrobe that helped her through her first few days in the country. Her place in Queenstown had private access with parking right outside the door. There was a king size bed, ensuite bathroom, and a living room with a sofa and table. There were no cooking facilities as it was a short walk to over 150 cafes, restaurants, and bars; however, there was a shared laundry space and a microwave.

Her South Island trip would start with some breathtaking views of Milford Sound. Followed by a stargazing trip in the much clearer sky of the southern hemisphere. There were completely different constellations and stars visible on this side of the planet, absolutely breathtaking.

Bridget had a long drive the following day. Her first stop was for the perfect social media post to capture the lone tree at Lake Wanaka. Everyone back home would be jealous about that. Bridget would include it in her Earth Day post every year after that. She circled the lake for an hour but couldn't find this tree. She should have done more research. *How big can this lake be? I'll surely see it once I'm there.* It was a much bigger lake than she planned for. She left without her picture and was ten minutes out from the lake, noticing all the hitchhikers on the side of the road when she thought, *I'll never be back here again, I might as well pull over and do some research and see if I can find it.* She turned around with a whole different body of knowledge and ended up getting the perfect social media picture of the lone tree.

On her way back to the car, she thought about all of those hitchhikers she passed. She read a lot of people do it in New Zealand and it was perfectly normal to visit this country with no plan or transportation in mind. Maybe she would pick up a couple of them on her way to Christchurch to help some fellow travelers. She had certainly been helped a few days ago and she wanted to pay the kindness forward. On second thought, absolutely not. She was there alone and could be easily carjacked or even worse. Maybe if she saw the right people, though, she would go for it.

As soon as she left the lake area, she spotted a man and a woman who looked to be about her age and thought, why not. There's a female there who wouldn't hurt her. She pulled over to the side of the road where they were.

"Where are you two heading?"

"Christchurch, mind if we ride along?"

"Why not, hop on in."

The female tried to enter the passenger's side, but Bridget had her things sprawled out across the passenger seat like she was living out of the car. They sat in the back after they put their luggage in the trunk.

"Hi, I'm Bridget from the United States. What are your names?"

"I'm Emma, from the Netherlands."

"I'm Otto, from Germany."

"Great to meet you both. Anywhere in particular I'm dropping you off at?"

"No plans really," Otto said. "We both came here without an itinerary and are going to most likely go our own way once we get to Christchurch. We met a couple of days ago and found out we had a mutual destination."

"We have such different ways of living in the United States."

They talked and talked about how things were different in their respective countries. She couldn't believe these two could take months of vacation time from their jobs when Bridget had spent all of her vacation time on this short three-week trip. There were rolling green hills as far as the eye could see in every direction that brought a peace to Bridget that she had never felt before. She was really starting to understand why those Hobbits chose to settle down in New Zealand and never wanted to leave the shire.

Bridget passed cars on the right her entire trip once she got more confident about driving on the wrong side of the road, and it made her passengers nervous every time she did it. Bridget thought about how they weren't staying together once they got to their destination and maybe one of them would like to hang out with her for the remainder of her trip.

She enjoyed the look in their eyes every single time she passed a car and would look back as soon as she maneuvered into oncoming traffic each time. She had their delicate little lives in the palm of her hand. There were long stretches of road with only one lane each way and the last car she attempted to pass was a semitruck which was moving slowly and didn't have a lot of visibility around it. Her car collided with an oncoming car when she tried to peek around the truck, which ejected her passengers straight through the windshield and into the New Zealand terrain. Bridget's airbag was no match for the combined force of her car and the one traveling at the same speed in the opposite direction. Bridget never even got to post her picture of the Lone Tree at Lake Wanaka.

England

(May 2018)

Russell was obsessed with the stock market. That was all his mind would be occupied with from the time he woke up in the morning, until the time he finally stopped looking at charts before he went to sleep. There wasn't a dip he didn't buy or a falling knife he couldn't catch when it came to the stock market. He spent all day every day at his boring government job reading news about the market and day trading in between whatever he was supposed to be doing as a government employee. If you asked him what he was supposed to be doing, he wouldn't even be able to make up an answer. Russell wasn't even sure how he was still on the payroll. It was like they had forgotten about him, and no one had ever questioned his role in this colossal hoodwinking machine he worked for.

Everything would be different next week though. Russell was heading to Gloucester in the United Kingdom to check out the annual cheese roll. He had seen the cheese roll on an ad on his trading app once and decided it was something he must do before he died. He was going to spend most of his time on this trip in London and venture out to see the infamous Stonehenge on his way to the festival. Two of his bucket list items would be crossed off the list in one.

London is the capital and largest city of the United Kingdom. It boasts the largest urban economy in Europe. This city attracts visitors from all over the world for its great higher educational systems and its overall influence on the global stage. This cosmopolitan area features some of the oldest pubs in the world as well as many modern attractions.

He was interested in seeing other things in a few other countries, but he was going to start traveling in a country which spoke his native language. Or at least a different version of the language Russell had been speaking since birth. Russell would see how this trip went and then consider his next country he would visit if he ever got the chance to.

Russell had been on a six-hour flight before when he traveled from his hometown of Atlanta to Seattle. However, this was his first international trip, and he was nervous about flying over the Atlantic Ocean. Hitting the water was somehow worse than hitting a mountain. Russell hadn't done a lot of research before he left for the trip. This research would superfluously cut into his stock market time. How would he sell the perfect covered call if his mind was occupied with other nefarious endeavors?

Russell and his wife Angela made it safely to London after a white knuckled take off and a butt clenching landing of a flight that experienced imperceptible turbulence on the way over. Russell and Angela walked by Westminster Abbey to see Big Ben, but he was not invigorated to see things he saw plenty of pictures of online. He promised Angela they would take a ride on the London Eye, and he was going to have to honor that commitment in two shakes of a lamb's tail.

"Did you remember to pack the international electrical outlet converters like I reminded you to do a hundred times?" Angela asked him.

"This is another reason why I don't travel," Russell replied. "And no, I didn't."

"Are you ever going to look up from that phone and appreciate this city around you that you have never been to before?"

"The OTC market is making a roaring comeback this year; I can feel it. We're going to retire early. Don't you want to retire early?"

"You've been saying this for years. It's two p.m. You said you were only going to be trading during the powers hour, or whatever you call it."

"With the time difference, the market opens at two thirty p.m. We're just about to get started with the opening power hour."

Angela let out a huge sigh. "Are you at least going to pick your head up for a few minutes to see the changing of the guards tomorrow?"

"That's earlier in the day before the market opens, I promise to check it out."

"You will be dragging me way out of town to see this stupid cheese rolling thing too. You better at least watch that."

"It's not stupid, and yes, I promise I won't use my phone the entire day."

They went to see the changing of the guard the following day, and Russell was mostly unimpressed. The only thing he could think about was all the market news he was missing out on. What would he do at the opening bell with incomplete information?

Russell was impressed at the tube system in London though. It was so efficient and takes you wherever you need to go without needing all of one's attention. The only downside was getting "Mind the gap" stuck in his mind for the rest of the trip.

"Why do people come to see the changing of the guard?" asked Russell.

"It's iconic!"

"It's boring. Why are they wearing those ridiculous clothes?"

"I, for one, love the pageantry of it."

"What does the royal family even do? I would be pissed if my tax dollars were being stolen to fund their extravagant lives without them producing anything."

"It's a tradition."

"And what was up with that breakfast this morning? Eggs with tomatoes and mushrooms and blood sausage. There are more chickens than people in this country and we're eating blood sausage? I don't know which one is stranger. The breakfast or the guard changing. They both want to make me puke."

The following day, they went to see Stonehenge on

their way out to Gloucester and Russell couldn't believe they had driven all the way out to the middle of nowhere for that.

"It took us hours to drive out here just to see a bunch of fairly large rocks?" Russell asked.

"Stonehenge was built thousands of years ago to track the sun, the moon, and the stars. It's quite impressive at the time it was built."

"Lame. We're in the middle of nowhere and the reception is garbage."

Angela gave him a scornful look.

"Oh, I'm sorry, it's *rubbish*," Russell said as he made air quotes with his fingers.

"Well, up next is your cheese rolling thing, so hopefully you're happy."

On Monday, they had finally made it to the famous Cooper's Hill to witness the cheese rolling ceremony. Contestants from all over the world flocked there once a year to line up at the top of the massive hill and chase a giant roll of cheese down the hill in an attempt to catch it. No one had ever caught up with the roll of cheese in the entire history of this event. Russell contemplated how much it would suck to be the first fatality of this event, as a result of getting rocked in the head by a big roll of cheese while observing the event at the bottom of the hill.

Angela and Russell stayed for the entire event watching wave after wave of hopeful contestants chase the cheese. Many people sprinted down the hill with a head full of steam like they had a chance and mostly walked away with cuts and bruises. There were a couple of broken bones that came with those who were determined and gave it their all. Moving slowly while leaning back on the butt technique appeared to be the safest option that Russell figured he would implement if he had ever returned to participate in the festivities. Russell spent the entire day off of his phone and had the time of his life watching the calamity take place.

They drove back to London after the event and Russell couldn't wipe the smile off his face as he ranted about all the funny wipeouts they witnessed. Especially the man whose shoes flung off immediately when he started at the top of the hill. Russell wasn't sure if the man even needed them as his bare feet might not have even met the Earth on the way down.

"I've never seen you this happy before. See what happens when you spend some time paying attention to the world around you?" Angela asked.

"That was incredible, we're going to have to come back here every year now," Russell replied.

"Maybe every other year. There are still so many other things to see on this wonderful planet."

"We'll see about that."

They dropped their rental car off the next day, and Russell was back to his usual stock market research on their way to the train station. Russell was walking to the train station and looked up and to the left of his phone before stepping into the street. The front of a double-decker bus, which did not attempt to touch the brakes, plowed into Russell, which sent him flying through the air. He was crossing the street at one of the many popular places where tourists cross and landed directly on top of the "LOOK RIGHT" writing in the middle of the street and bled out internally.

Russell drove on the left side of the road the entire previous day, but he was too wrapped up in his greed to remember to look in the opposite direction of traffic he was used to while crossing the road. Angela, who looked both ways, ended up retiring early on one of Russell's penny stocks which skyrocketed the following week.

Germany

(September 2017)

The amount of beer drank at Oktoberfest each year can fill more than three Olympic-sized swimming pools. In September of each year, people travel hundreds and thousands of miles to drink beer in liter increments and to make new friends from all over the globe. Nothing has brought people together throughout history more than this delicious nectar from the gods. It has also been known to start a lot of fights, but not inside the tents of the Theresienwiese Garden in Munich.

Oktoberfest is the largest gathering of drunkards and beer enthusiasts around the world. To many folks, if those two groups of people were represented in a Venn diagram, it would look like a circle. Connor considered himself just a beer enthusiast, though.

James, Connor, and Vic entered the fairgrounds for their second day of beer consumption, which would begin with some hair of the dog to heal the wounds of yesterday. They wanted to get there early to make sure they would be able to get a seat before every table was reserved. Getting a table at Oktoberfest was much easier than they expected. They were solely looking for abatement of their hangover symptoms.

The massive white tents littering the fairgrounds were only called tents because of their appearance. They were huge permanent structures that could house thousands of beer enthusiasts each and some even have an additional floor that lined the inside perimeter. The group learned the previous day to stay out of the way of the servers or they would pinch you so hard and yell at you to make you never get in the way of them making their money ever again. A server had just ushered them to their first table of the day.

"Drei Bier!" Connor said confidently to the server as he held up his index finger, middle finger, and thumb. The German way to signal three. She nodded and stormed off to grab their three giant mugs of brew.

"You're really getting the hang of this German thing," James said jokingly.

"Now that I have that down and already knew wunderbar before the trip, I now know three German words. I think I'm ready to apply for citizenship."

"Whatever you have to do to help us come back here every year for the rest of our lives. This place is what I imagine heaven is like."

"I still feel like we aren't fitting in until we buy some lederhosen."

"Maybe we can rent some, that stuff is way too heavy and luggage-space consuming to bring it back with us."

"Did you know the original Oktoberfest was to celebrate a wedding?"

"I would marry this place if I could."

"Also, the drinking age here is sixteen. I wish I would have grown up here."

The server came back with their three liter-sized beers along with a few other folks who appeared to be from the United States. They paid for their beers and the waitress walked away after asking the other group of three guys what they wanted. Connor thought about using the German words he knew to order their new guests a few beers, but he didn't know them well enough yet. Maybe he would have built up the courage if he had already had a few beers.

"What's up? What are your names?" Connor asked the new people at their table.

"I'm Nick, and this is Andrew and Kody. How about y'all?"

Connor noticed they had a northern United States accent, however, they were using words people in the south typically used.

"I'm Connor, and this is James and Vic. Nice to meet you three."

"We had two others in our group, Eric and Tyler. They went too hard yesterday though. They'll probably be catching up with us in another chapter later on."

"I know that struggle. We all made it back today, surprisingly."

"This is our first stop on our European trip. We got

slightly overzealous last night. We're heading to Amsterdam after this, and then London for the American football game," said Nick.

"Nice! I've always wanted to see Wembley stadium. We're only here for Oktoberfest and to do more exploring in the countryside. I mostly wanted to drink my weight in beer and drive on the autobahn while I'm over here. Not at the same time of course."

"That probably wouldn't be a great idea."

"What is your favorite part about Oktoberfest?"

"Besides the girls wearing their dirndls? I'm amazed at this powdery substance they're selling out in the open. They say it isn't cocaine, it looks exactly like cocaine though."

"If it looks like a duck, and smells like a duck, it must be cocaine. There are so many varieties out there, though. Everyone seems to have their own blend of what seems to be kitchen spices and other things they're snorting."

"I don't get it. I guess it's a display of strength or something."

"Who knows," Connor said. "I'll probably get drunk enough at some point to want to display my strength. How about y'all? What is your favorite part?"

"The troughs in the men's water closets are interesting, not that I'm looking around a bunch while I'm in the bathroom or anything. I would have to say the hill that everyone goes to afterward is a spectacle."

"The hill?" Connor asked.

"Everyone goes out near the Bavarian Statue afterwards and pees and vomits and does whatever else they need to do after the tents close. It's exhilarating."

"I think we'll have to check that out and see whatever else they're doing."

The guys finished their beers and never ended up meeting the two missing members of their new friend group. Perhaps they would run into them again in another tent or walking around the fairgrounds later. They were on a strict schedule and couldn't wait around to meet people they would probably never see again. Connor had the lofty goal of drinking a beer in every single tent inside the Oktoberfest fairgrounds. There was no way any human could achieve a goal like that in the amount of time they had without a liver transplant.

The day went on and they knocked out a couple of other tents on their list and met some new friends from Russia and Brazil. The group went on some of the amusement park rides they didn't realize were there before they stepped foot on the fairgrounds. They ate schnitzel and giant pretzels big enough to wear around their necks and tapped out before they could make it to the hill afterwards.

The crew reconvened the following morning and weren't completely sure how they got home the previous night. They attempted to put together the missing pieces after they found a receipt that proved they made the last train home to their hotel the night before. They left the festival way before the last train home. What happened in between? They may have been completely annihilated, regardless, they always made their way back to safety when they needed to. Especially in a foreign land.

Connor had devised a secret plan before they left the United States. He found these pills online which could be taken the night before with some food and it would alleviate the symptoms of a hangover. He could keep up with his two friends back home whenever they were drinking. However, he would wake up with a hangover the next morning and be completely bedridden the entire following day. Regretfully, he had forgotten to follow this routine the night before and had a mind-crushing migraine. They had all planned to venture out into the countryside on this day; their splitting headaches would encourage them otherwise. They all decided to nap a while and see if it would change their situation.

The crew woke up again at the early time of one thirty p.m. in their elegant two-bedroom apartment located near Josephsburg subway station. Josephsburg was a U-Bahn station in Munich on the U2 line. They needed to take the subway three stops to Hauptbahnhof central station then the U4/U5 one stop to get to Oktoberfest. It was a great location to get to Theresienwiese and most other places in Munich easily. They loved how easy it was to use public transportation there, both sober and while absolutely hammered.

Their place featured a living room combined with a kitchen, one bathroom, and two balconies. They all became acquainted with the German poop shelf styled toilet that morning. Their place was older and equipped with toilets which didn't have the traditional standing water at the bottom of the bowl. Instead, there was a shelf of porcelain that would catch any deposits and a flush would cause a riptide of furious water to sweep anything standing in its path. A courtesy flush and overall expeditiousness were imperative in this situation, as any deposit would sit stale in the breathable air.

They decided they were wasting their vacation at their place and would fight through the debilitating hangover. Connor scheduled a rental car for one day and they were going to make use of it while they were in the land of unlimited speed limits.

The crew wandered around their apartment they were staying at aimlessly, like zombies without a living human to chase. No one spoke to each other, as they needed to concentrate their entire efforts into making themselves presentable to head out into the world. They carefully walked down the stairs of their building, holding onto the railing at all times to keep themselves from tumbling down each step. Connor was behind the others and could see their legs trembling like baby giraffes taking their first steps with every stair they descended.

The other two guys grabbed a bite to eat at the convenience store located below their apartment, but Connor wasn't able to eat yet. Even Currwurst, his favorite meal, didn't look appetizing at the moment. Connor considered getting a beer which always helped his situation. Beer is food in Germany, right? He only bought a soda and hoped the carbonation would release some of the knots in his stomach so he would be able to eat.

After a long struggle to get ready and maintain their

composure at the car rental counter, they were in their mid-grade sedan and pulling out onto the autobahn outside of Munich. They decided on a slight car upgrade due to their budget restrictions; Connor wanted something with extra gumption to take full advantage of these perfectly maintained German roads.

"Can we go as fast as we want to on any road?" Connor asked.

"You are driving us around and you don't know the rules here?" replied Vic.

"I got my international driving permit before I came here. I'm qualified in the eyes of the law."

"You amaze me sometimes with the lack of planning you put into these trips."

"There is a ton of construction here. It makes sense because these roads are perfect. Knowing the signs would definitely help."

"From what I read, whenever there is a sign with four lines going through it diagonally, there basically aren't any rules."

Connor moved his hand horizontally above his eyes as if scanning off on the horizon.

"Look at that, there's my sign."

Connor stomped his right foot all the way to the floor with the accelerator beneath it. Pedal to the metal, as they say. It was a thrill to see the speedometer fly through the numbers in kilometers instead of miles per hour. Before Connor knew it, he was already going two hundred kilometers per hour, whatever that translated to in miles per hour. Connor looked in the rearview mirror and saw a car frantically flashing his headlights and approaching them like they were standing still. He felt as if it were a road rage situation but was assuming the light flashing was etiquette for him to get out of the way. This headache of his was devitalizing his reaction time.

He swerved to the next lane, narrowly missing a driver who wasn't going as fast as he could possibly go, and noticed the car in the left lane flashing his hazard lights as he passed. Was he thanking Connor for moving over?

"Are you trying to kill us? Slow down! There was another sign without the lines," Vic said.

"What does that mean?" asked Connor.

"I'm assuming it means you can't drive however fast you want to anymore."

"That guy was doing it even faster."

They all screamed when they noticed the concrete barriers in front of them, which was shifting them all the way across the median and into the other side of the highway. Connor slammed on the brakes barely in time to fit into the much narrower lane, then swooped over the median to the other side of the highway.

"You almost killed us!" Vic yelled.

"I knew exactly what I was doing."

"No more driving as fast as you want when you see the four-line signs, unless we pull over and memorize what the signage means in this country."

"Alright, you win," Connor said.

"This near-death experience has really made me hungry."

"That makes one of us."

"You haven't even eaten yet today, have you?"

"It's strange, it's how my body works, I guess."

The three of them pulled back into the rental car parking lot and were back in the office, returning the keys to the car they had pushed to the limits that day. They had a brief need for speed and wouldn't need the car for the full twenty-four hours they had reserved it for.

"How did the car treat you?" the rental representative asked Connor.

"Oh me? Yeah, it was fine."

Connor looked around the room, seemingly evaluating his next steps. Connor's headache had consumed most of his mental functioning after their near-death experience.

"Can I have the keys?"

Connor got a weird dizzy feeling he had when he first woke up before his nap. He ignored it since the most dangerous part of their day had passed and he could get through anything life would throw at him at this point.

"Sir? The keys?"

He was not able to hear what the rental agent was saying as he moved his mouth. Connor's eyes rolled into the back of his head, and he had a seizure right at the counter as a result of an alcohol withdrawal. He smacked his head on the counter on the way down, which ruptured a blood vessel in his brain, and never made the plane back to the United States a few days later. He wasn't even close to achieving his goal of drinking a beer in every tent at Oktoberfest that year.

Netherlands

(September 2017)

"Our host told us that the key would be to the left of the front door," Nick said.

Nick and his friends inspected the small entryway which had the address for their second accommodation of the trip posted on the door.

"The place is on a busy street. How could it possibly be to the left of the door? Not even in a lockbox or anything?" Tyler asked.

"The host didn't provide a code to unlock any sort of lockbox."

"Are you sure this is the correct place?"

"One hundred percent."

"I'm no mathematician, but this sure doesn't look like one hundred percent."

"He isn't messaging me back either. I guess we can explore the town a little with our luggage."

Nick kicked a crumpled-up ball of paper in the left corner of the entryway. "Hold on a minute." He walked out into the sidewalk to retrieve the wad of paper he had sent flying and unraveled the balled-up mess. "Found the keys!"

They filed into the place after Nick struggled to turn the key and climbed the extremely steep and narrow stairs to their third story room in Amsterdam. Where else would a group of guys go for a stag party after a brief few days at Oktoberfest in Germany, and before seeing their favorite American football team play across the pond in London?

This was the second apartment they booked as their first host canceled a week before they left the United States. What a shock. They wanted to stay on one of the many houseboats while they were there, although there were too many of them in their group for that. Their studio apartment had a single bedroom with five twin beds and a tiny single bathroom attached to it. The place featured chic flooring throughout and contemporary furniture with a kitchenette to make tea and coffee.

They all took turns showering the airport stink off of them while the others dreamed up all the possible scenarios of how the night would proceed. Nick's strategy would be to get as intoxicated as possible to drown out the other four guys snoring all night in this single bedroom. He was just happy he wasn't on another top bunk bed this time around.

Technically speaking, marijuana wasn't legal in public in this beautiful country. This didn't stop the millions of residents and tourists from partaking in the drug found in most "coffee shops."

These stags were finally ready and shopped all their

options at the store closest to their accommodations. They headed back to indulge in their purchases in the comfort of a private location. They bought a nice sativa strain to prevent them from absorbing into the couch for the rest of the night. They still wanted to explore the town and didn't want to waste the opportunity for a fresh hunt in a foreign land.

"Let's get a nice wholesome activity in before we start gallivanting around town tonight. Any ideas?" asked Nick.

"Speaking of wholesome, did you see all of those windmills on the flight in?" asked Eric.

"They were lovely. How about a nice canal tour?"

"We can do that. Amsterdam is sinking more into the ocean every year though; we need to commence the gallivanting before it's gone."

There was a canal perpendicular to the street they were staying on and only a few houses away. The crew didn't have the funds to stay right on the canal. They could barely see it from their third-floor window if they looked at just the right angle. If Nick got on his tippy toes, he could see the bridge crossing over the canal, which was littered with unlocked bikes on each side of the bridge's fencing.

The romantic canals were slightly overshadowed by the brown murky water which reminded Nick of the grotesque soupy liquid back home in the Baltimore Harbor. There wasn't a lot of trash in these waters though, no need for a Mr. Trash Wheel here. He remembered a news article about a group of tourists that visited his hometown the previous year who had went for a swim in the harbor. Needless to say, they needed all kinds of shots to protect them from who knows what kind of diseases lived in the harbor, filled with trash and human bodies. Nick would make sure that he didn't end up in the water here in Amsterdam.

The canal had a lane of car traffic on either side of it going in opposite directions, with room to park cars on each side of the lanes. The cars parked closest to the canal were only a few feet from the edge and Nick realized why a lot of people decided to ride bicycles instead of automobiles. He wasn't the best at parallel parking and knew he would send his car into the water after barely passing that part of the test when he got his driver's license.

Nick was walking in front of his groomsmen and took a step out into the road before being almost annihilated by a speeding bicyclist. The bicyclist looked back and gave him the old one finger salute.

"First time in Amsterdam?" a random stranger, who was leaning up against a light pole nearby, asked.

"Yes, what was up with that?"

"Bicyclists control the roads over here, you need to be attentive before you cross the street, making sure to look both ways. There's three times as many bikes as cars here and sixty percent of people ride a bicycle every day."

"If bikes are so sacred around here, why aren't any of them attached and locked up to anything?"

"Most everyone that lives here has two bicycles. They have a nice one they keep at home and only take it out for special occasions where it won't get stolen."

"And the other bike?"

"They have a cheaper bike that gets them from point A to point B. No one locks them up because there are so many bikes and they might get stolen."

"So, they have to use their expensive bike if it gets stolen?"

"No, they steal someone else's."

"Sounds like a great system."

"Enjoy the rest of your time here."

It wasn't hard to find folks who spoke English but it didn't seem like there was any one language that everyone spoke. It was a mixture of languages and accents from every country surrounding it. There was a slight majority of people speaking Dutch, which was particularly harsh on the ears.

They walked around assessing all the boats that could take them around town through the canals and judged them based on two criteria. The first was the number of women who were on the boat. The second was if they were serving alcoholic beverages. They found the perfect guide that met both of these prerequisites two blocks away from their place.

"Let's have a couple beers here, then we can head back to the place and partake in some of the products we bought at the coffee shop. Then we'll head back out into the town for some action."

"Sounds like a plan."

"We'll end the night in the red-light district," said Eric.

"Not me, I'm getting married soon," said Nick.

"Everyone will participate in the red light special. We

all need to be complicit to share in this collective guilt and be sworn to secrecy."

"That's terrible logic."

"It's mind over matter, and I don't have a mind, so it doesn't matter."

Eric was speaking the truth there.

The boat tour guide was speaking and they weren't paying attention to him. "Notice the ladders which are placed periodically throughout the canals, most people who fall in don't have a great chance of surviving, but the ladders have saved people."

"How about a blue light then?" asked Tyler.

"What's the deal with a blue light?" asked Nick.

"They're half off, red lighters that have come upon hard times."

"Don't let them do that to you," a stranger interjected.

"Do what to me?" Nick asked.

"The ones with the blue lights usually have extra parts down there," the man said as he pointed to his crotch. "If you know what I mean. Not that there's anything wrong with that."

"C'mon man, we almost gave Nick the bachelor party experience of a lifetime."

They got back to the dock and after walking on dry land for a minute, they realized they were still walking like they had been trying to maintain their balance out on the water. They didn't stand up much on the boat and those drinks started to take effect. They noticed a sign for a peep show and couldn't resist the urge to explore more of the native culture.

Everyone in the crew entered the building apprehensively and walked along the curved wall which had a bunch of doors that were open and available. Nick jumped into the first booth, locked the door behind himself, and looked around to figure out what the deal was. There was a full schedule posted on the wall with the sequence of events taking place in the center room which was surrounded by these booths. The times were all listed using the twenty-four-hour clock which always gave Nick some trouble. Take the hour and subtract by twelve if it is above twelve, he told himself. After some complex calculations, Nick realized he was early for the girl-on-girl performance; he would have to settle for a solo show.

He purchased a minute for a peek before deciding to dedicate more money for an entire ten minutes. There was a plethora of coins in his pocket he had collected from the countries who used the euro. At least the coins could get you somewhere over in Europe instead of the useless denominations in the United States. Nick usually ended up tossing coins in a random tip jar or charity collection container. Every country needs to start using the euro, Nick thought. He waded through the sea of shrapnel in his pocket, placed his money in the slot, and the window opened to the center of the circular room where the performance was taking place. He couldn't believe this was something so easy and cheap to see live.

He quickly noticed the other windows that lined the center room where all of his friends were waving and pointing at each other and making inappropriate gestures. Tyler appeared to be shoving something phallic into his mouth while poking his cheek out with his tongue. Eric was poking his index finger into a circle formed by his other index finger and thumb. There was some breast squeezing motions and squeezing their own chests together. This was exactly why he and his friends could never have nice things, silly Americans.

Later in the night, after a few different bars and more coffee products, they finally saw it.

"Look, there it is! The red-light district," Eric said and gazed down the street with wonder in his eyes.

"I'm not going down there," Nick said.

"Nothing wrong with a little window shopping, you're going with us. We are a wolf pack and we will not be separated."

Tyler and Eric grabbed his arms and forced him down the street with them. They walked along the vast network of doors which featured every type of woman imaginable, gawking at everyone they encountered. Nick looked around and saw everyone else doing the same exact thing, pathetic.

"This is your girl here; she has the features I know you enjoy up top."

Nick dug his heels in. "I'm not going in there."

"What are you afraid of?" the lovely blonde with the nice features up top asked.

"It's my stag party and I will not be thinking about this on my wedding day," Nick replied.

"We can have a nice conversation then; it'll make your friends happy."

Eric and Tyler shoved him inside and slammed the

door shut.

"Hi, what's your name?" Nick awkwardly asked.

"I'm Linda." She handed him the list of services she provided with the associated prices. "And you are?"

"Um." He forgot his name for a second as she bent over to grab a condom he knocked off the desk in his hasty entry. "Nick! That's it, I'm Nick."

"Where are you from, Nick?"

"Baltimore. I have a lovely fiancée who is from Baltimore too. And I can't wait to see her after this."

"I don't see her here right now."

Linda ran a finger down his chest.

The turmoil of what happens in Amsterdam stays in Amsterdam burned fiercely inside of him. The twelve beers and still lingering effects of the "coffee" products were starting to win the fight against his strong resilience to stay faithful. Linda's finger was now down teasing the inseam of his pants.

"So which service are you interested in? I'll even knock off fifty percent for the special occasion."

"I guess no one will know, right?"

Linda unbuttoned his pants and placed the condom on him like it was not her first rodeo, and Nick was sure this wasn't her first ten rodeos either. She began riding him like this wasn't her first one hundred rodeos. Nick could only think about his fiancée as she was putting on the performance of a lifetime, and the immense guilt turned his noodle al dente.

"Don't think about it, live in the moment."

"Please stop," Nick said in the politest way he could

muster. "Nothing against you, you're gorgeous. And you have all the right motions. I keep thinking about what a horrible mistake this was. I love my fiancée."

"It happens with a lot of folks from the States, they aren't built for fun like us Europeans. That'll be forty euros."

"Even with the discount?"

"I have kids to feed." Linda held her hand out.

Nick left Linda feeling extremely remorseful. He was steadfast on being faithful to his fiancée all day and failed when it was most important for him to stick with his morals. He lost his last forty euros and lost all respect for himself at the same time.

Nick couldn't find any of his other friends in the surrounding area and assumed they were all following through with their commitment to the collective guilt. Tears welled up into his eyes as he sulked his way over to the ATM down by the canal. He could barely see where he was going and placed his foot over the edge of the road and went tumbling down end over end into the water. His pants got snagged in the wall on the way down and almost saved him, but ended up getting ripped apart. No one was around to see him fall in. He tried to scream for help and his mouth just filled up with water. He clawed at the walls lining the canal not knowing there was a ladder thirty feet away from him that would have saved his life.

The other guys all met up after their experiences and waited thirty minutes before knocking on Linda's door to see if he was still having the time of his life in there. They looked around for another hour before heading back to the place to see if he went back early. They found his body in the water near the red-light district the following morning with the rubber still wrapped around his willy.

Hungary

(September 2017)

The wedding was only two months away, and it was time for Claire and the ladies to have their one last hen party. It was not even a debate; she and the ladies would be heading to Budapest, Hungary, for some last-minute action before she tied the knot. Would they meet up with a stag party visiting from London and pair off some other their single friends for the night? Maybe they would just throw all their belongings in a circle to dance around and stick to themselves the whole time? Would they get harassed by a bunch of uninteresting men who didn't speak the same language as them and go home sadly disappointed? Maybe they would combine powers and summon the dark lord Cthulhu? Who knew! The possibilities were endless.

Claire wasn't too concerned about one thing leading to another since her fiancé, Nick, and his idiotic pals were off partying in Amsterdam. The land where things illuminated by red lights or blue lights were purchased effortlessly. Claire imagined Nick's stupid friend Tyler being pushed into the canal after getting into a bar brawl, as they always did. There were ladders everywhere in the canal for those types of situations. He'd be fine.

The place they rented out was a bright and airy, recently renovated three-bedroom apartment which could sleep up to six people. The apartment was fully furnished. It featured cable TV, wireless internet access, and had authentic original parquet floors. All three bedrooms were fully air-conditioned. There were two large bedrooms fitted with king-sized beds and leather sofas, and the third bedroom with a double bed and a small sofa. The apartment had a street facing balcony, large bright windows, high ceilings, and modern fittings throughout the two and a half bathrooms. The kitchen was well equipped with a dining table for six people, a microwave, a big fridge, and a dishwasher.

Claire picked Budapest so she and the ladies could relax in the famous Széchenyi thermal bath and maybe visit some of the other 1,500 spas in Hungary before the wedding activities stressed her out over the coming months. The main reason they were in Budapest was for the ruin bar scene. The idea of a ruin bar is simple. Find an old, abandoned building, preferably with a courtyard, rent it out, and fill it with a bunch of random art and junk following a general theme. All of this done tastefully provided the perfect party atmosphere. They all have their own themes and collectively offered an endless variety of different drinking environments to explore.

Claire and the ladies would explore the artsy low-key spots during the day, and hit the largest ruin bar later each night. The largest establishment was more of a complex which featured a variety of different themed areas connected through a labyrinth of different hallways. Each of them had picked their favorite theme in this network of bars before the trip, and they would spend most of their time each night in their favorite spot on their assigned day. Under no circumstances were they to go off on their own during this vacation.

The bar they were currently in had a music and plant vibe going on. Claire was never an animal person, and wasn't sure about having children either, so her plants back home were her babies. There was the shell of an old piano in the corner of the courtyard, with hop vines extending from inside of it and up the entire wall. Brass instruments hung from the railings of the balcony which ran around half of the second level. A standup bass with no strings stood in another corner of the courtyard. The staff had attached plant hangers to the ceilings below the balconies and large floor potted plants were everywhere the eye could see.

"Did Molly make it along for the trip?" Claire asked.

None of the ladies were, in fact, named Molly.

"She was safe and sound in my checked bag the entire time," Julie replied.

"This is going to be quite a week to remember, or not remember."

"You've never had any drugs besides alcohol, right?"

"That's right, I'm going to live it up and get this out of my system before married life ends all the fun."

"You'll just have to include your fiancé in these activities now."

"His company drug tests him constantly. He's too uptight and would never participate in these activities. I know him."

"What about when Nick retires?"

"Well, maybe then, but that's decades from now and I'm not waiting that long to experiment. Tonight, is the night."

"Cheers to that."

"To our fiancés, to our boyfriends, and to praying they never meet."

They all raised their glasses of sauvignon blanc and slammed them together before downing whatever amount of liquid they each had left.

"Before we head to the next spot, there's this statue I really wanted to check out," Cindy said.

"A statue? I didn't come here for sightseeing. If it makes you happy, I guess we can check it out. What is the statue?" Claire asked.

Cindy looked down at her phone. "The statue of András Hadik." She struggled to read the name of the statue.

"You don't even remember what it was called and you want to see it that bad?"

"Hear me out. It's a giant statue of a horse that is a good ten feet off of the ground. People come from all over to climb the thing and rub its balls for good luck."

"Cindy, you make it so difficult to love you sometimes. Last year, you brought us all the way to Belgium to see a statue of a boy holding his little penis. Another statue of a girl peeing in an alleyway. And to wrap it all up, a dog with a massive penis in the middle of peeing on a bollard in the sidewalk."

"You have to admit, the dog penis was impressive for the size of the dog."

"I'm not admitting anything. What is it with you and other species penises and balls?"

"Hey, I like to acknowledge a good penis when I see it, even if it's another species."

"Sick. You even ordered a rooster testicle and cock comb soup when you got here. Why couldn't you order goulash like a normal person?" Claire asked.

"Wait until I make you all go to the penis museum in Iceland with me."

"Nope, not happening."

"Just give me this one. It's apparently good luck and we could all use it if we're going to get lucky tonight."

"Whatever you say," Claire said. "Lead the way."

They walked block after block. The buzz from the wine earlier was wearing off, and they were all starting to wonder if their trek was worth it. The statue wasn't nearly as close as Cindy was leading on when they were all sitting around earlier.

"Where is this thing?" Claire asked.

"One more block, I swear," Cindy replied. "Did you know Budapest was originally named after the two separate areas that are split by the beautiful Danube River? We're on the rich side now, Buda, and we'll be pests later, on the Pest side of town."

"Don't try to distract us. I bet you are the only person in the world who thinks this is good luck."

"The entire internet says it's good luck. Everything on

the internet is true."

"If it isn't actually one more block away, then I'm heading to the closest bar and buying everyone palinka. It may taste like rubbing alcohol that's been in the same room as whatever fruit it's supposed to taste like for a day, but it's better than this."

They rounded the corner and stumbled upon an entire tour group standing around the horse statue. The tour guide even brought his own step stool, and they were all scaling the structure one at a time to rub the horse's testicles.

"See!" Cindy exclaimed. "It's a thing. Everyone knows it's good luck."

"Holy balls, look at the size of those things. It's like one of those Botero sculptures we saw in Colombia where certain features are exaggerated beyond belief."

They waited their turn in line behind the tour group to get a look at these coconuts that were in fact impressive, like the dog statue Cindy had led them to in Belgium the previous year. The testicles on the horse were also a completely different shade than the rest of the statue, due to the amount of people who had handled them over the years.

Claire was first in line as the wife to be and scaled the base of the statue. They didn't bring a nice nifty step stool with them to assist, and the other tour guide was well on their way to their next stop before they got their turn. Claire was at the top of the cement base of the monument and had her arm around the horse's leg when she got dizzy from the height and climbed back down to safety.

"Were they too big to handle?" asked Cindy.

"They were just too beautiful." Claire masked the fact that she was embarrassed.

Everyone else took their turns handling the horse testicles as the others hooted and hollered when each of them made contact. Everyone got a nice rub besides Claire.

After drinking at a couple more ruin bars and an early evening nap, they were ready for the first big night of mayhem to ensue. They wore the dresses they promised their partners they wouldn't bring but secretly packed anyway. Their makeup was perfect thanks to Julie, who was providing her makeup services for the upcoming wedding as well. They gathered around each other and Julie brought out the aspirin bottle which was no longer filled with aspirin and passed it around to everyone.

"Blast off," Claire said.

"Party mode engaged," Julie added.

The group left their apartment and walked into the front door of the largest ruin bar in Budapest. They knew exactly where they were going from the months of research and online forums they studied of the network of bars inside the complex.

They passed the initial dance floor when they walked in, which featured a nautical theme that played exclusively nineties American throwback jams. The crew proceeded into the first hallway of many. Next was another dance floor with a jungle vibe playing dubstep originating from Europe. They thought the jungle theme might be too much for Claire's first time consuming hallucinogens.

They were finally in their last hallway before reaching the room they planned for. A room inspired by heaven which was perfect for these goddesses. They played whatever the billboard top 100 hits were at the time. There were puffy clouds and those baby angels scattered everywhere around the room. Claire thought, what were those baby angels called? Cherubs? She was well on her way to cloud nine though and wasn't confident about a lot of things.

"This is cool and all, however, I think I want to go exploring a little more," Claire said.

"Well, someone should go with you. Not me, someone else. This is the room I picked out and I'm staying here. Not it," Cindy replied, as she held her pointer finger to her nose.

"Alright, I'll go with her," Julie finally said after everyone was already touching their noses.

Julie and Claire were feeling adventurous with the help of their aspirin bottle contents, and felt like they had been exploring for an eternity. Room after hallway after room after hallway. This ruin bar never seemed to end. They felt like they were in an IKEA that kept bringing you back to the beginning instead of eventually ending up at the checkout.

Every time Claire thought she couldn't imagine this place having another theme, she discovered another completely new and interesting world. They didn't even realize they had been circling the same four rooms for an entire hour, wading through the crowds of other people who were also under the influence of outside forces.

"I think that guy gave me a look. I'm going to go talk

to him," Julie said with googly eyes.

Claire didn't even hear what Julie said and replied, "I'm going to try to find a bathroom."

"They're called water closets here!" Julie yelled as Claire walked off.

Claire was already gone before she could hear Julie's reply. She searched and searched but couldn't find a bathroom or restroom sign anywhere and panicked when she realized she had no idea where she had parted ways with Julie. Maybe what Julie said as they parted could have helped her.

Was Julie in the jungle room? No, that was days ago. Wait, they hadn't even been in town for more than a day. Was she in the space themed room? Was there even a space themed room or was she imagining it? Claire's heart beat faster and faster as she got paranoid about the pills they had consumed. She was trying it out for the first time as her bladder was pleading with her to find a bathroom. The music was bumping, and the crowd of people all seemed like they were towering over her and talking about her. She finally saw a door and ran over to it and slammed it shut behind her to get away from everyone.

The room was completely dark except for the faint light from the dance floor outlining the door. She felt around for a light switch and realized it was a tiny room since she could touch all four walls without moving her feet. No light switch. Claire decided she would have to go back out and fight the sea of people. She found the door handle and twisted; however, the door was locked. She was trapped, alone.

She tried to calm herself down and could now feel her pulse in every inch of her body, as if the vibrations from the music weren't enough. *It's just the drugs*, she thought. Claire attempted to start problem solving and felt around to try to determine if there was anything in the closet that could help her get out. She could feel a rectangular plastic object with a handle and wheels attached to it, a mop bucket! This was a janitor's closet. She rammed the bucket into the door as she screamed as loud as she could.

"Someone please, anyone!"

No one outside could hear her pounding on the door to the beat of the sweet bass sound coming out of the speakers. Her heart rate was still steadily increasing. *At least I can relieve myself in the mop bucket*, she thought. What if she was trapped in here for a while? She felt extremely dehydrated from the drinking they all had participated in earlier. There was no way she was going to survive on dirty mop water.

"Help! Someone please, help!"

She pounded on the door again. Claire's heart rate reached dangerous levels as her bladder screamed. She felt an acute tightness in her chest as her consciousness of the world around her slipped away. The perfect combination of fear and drug use overwhelmed her heart as the lights around the door faded into nothingness.

Her friends went home that night thinking Claire probably went home with a guy as one last joy ride before the big wedding day, no judgment there. The workers at the ruin bar would only discover her body after a stench far worse than a janitor's closet seeped out from inside. They found Claire hiding in the darkness, embracing her rectangular yellow mop bucket.

SAFE TRAVELS!

AUTHOR'S NOTE:

Everyone always talks to me about all the wonderful places I have visited outside of the United States and it always leads to the same question: I know you would probably rather live anywhere besides here, which country was your favorite? There are positives and negatives everywhere in the world and most people are mostly annoyed with the problems that would exist wherever they live. I have spent a limited amount of time in each country drinking and galivanting everyday so of course they all seemed great. It's hard to pick an absolute favorite, I can definitely provide a top three or top five, but there is nowhere else I would rather live than the United States.

First and foremost, I have to thank one of my best friends Josh, who has accompanied me on most of these trips and for the most part planned them. Next up, his father Vic, who birthed him and went on the first international trip I ever went on to Iceland. Other notable mentions on other trips, in no particular order: Sam, Charles, Rashad, other Vic, Billy, Tim, Holly, Gina, other Josh, Gino, random hitchhikers I picked up in New Zealand, Nicole, Eric, Tyler, Karl, Cindy, Kelsey, Andrea, Joe, random swingers in Canada, Summer, Kendall, Damian, and Carlyn. Special shout out to Summer who reads like 200 books a year and gave me feedback on my manuscripts within hours of me sending them to her.

The memories I've created with these incredible people were the inspiration for this book and I wouldn't trade my experiences with these fine folks for anything material that exists on this planet we call Earth. I won one of the greatest lotteries being born in the United States and am grateful for having a passport which gains me access to most parts of the world. The last shoutout goes to my girlfriend Kaitlin, who gave me plenty of time to work on this book while she studied for her EPPP, which she passed.

I'm going to end this book similarly to every walking tour outro I've heard on the many free walking tours I've been on over the years: If you've enjoyed this book, please leave me a review on Amazon and/or Goodreads and if you're a fan of Sci-Fi check out my other book *The Hypersleep Chronicles*. If you didn't like this book you're reading, the title of this book is *Neither Here nor There* by Bill Bryson.

Made in the USA
Monee, IL
03 September 2024